Fariq frowned dow... *...your as his chest rose and fell, his breathing uneven. "You are full of surprises," he said. "As passionate and bright and mysterious as the desert."*

Her heart was racing and her pulse pounded in her ears. She didn't know what to say. "Fariq, I—"

He let out a long breath as he touched the rim of her sunglasses. "My little jewel of the desert…let me see your eyes."

He was going to take off her glasses? Suddenly adrenaline rushed through her, putting her mental circuits back online. She backed away from him, out of the circle of his arms. Her skin was clear of everything but sunscreen. Not a speck of makeup. But her hair was hanging around her face and she didn't have on her long, shapeless clothes. Sunglasses were the only part of her disguise in place, her last defense.

And defense was definitely what she needed.

ᴅESERT ᴮRIDES

Dear Reader,

If you're like me, you can't get enough heartwarming love stories and real-life fairy tales that end happily ever after. You'll find what you need and so much more with Silhouette Romance each month.

This month you're in for an extra treat. Bestselling author Susan Meier kicks off MARRYING THE BOSS'S DAUGHTER—the brand-new six-book series written exclusively for Silhouette Romance. In this launch title, *Love, Your Secret Admirer* (#1684), our favorite matchmaking heiress helps a naive secretary snare her boss's attention with an eye-catching makeover.

A sexy rancher discovers love and the son he never knew, when he matches wits with a beautiful teacher, in *What a Woman Should Know* (#1685) by Cara Colter. And a not-so plain Jane captures a royal heart, in *To Kiss a Sheik* (#1686) by Teresa Southwick, the second of three titles in her sultry DESERT BRIDES miniseries.

Debrah Morris brings you a love story of two lifetimes, in *When Lightning Strikes Twice* (#1687), the newest paranormal love story in the SOULMATES series. And sparks sizzle between an innocent curator—with a big secret—and the town's new lawman, in *Ransom* (#1688) by Diane Pershing. Will a seamstress's new beau still love her when he learns she is an undercover heiress? Find out in *The Bridal Chronicles* (#1689) by Lissa Manley.

Be my guest and feed your need for tender and lighthearted romance with all six of this month's great new love stories from Silhouette Romance.

Enjoy!

Mavis C. Allen
Associate Senior Editor, Silhouette Romance

Please address questions and book requests to:
Silhouette Reader Service
U.S.: 3010 Walden Ave., P.O. Box 1325, Buffalo, NY 14269
Canadian: P.O. Box 609, Fort Erie, Ont. L2A 5X3

To Kiss a Sheik

TERESA SOUTHWICK

DESERT BRIDES

SILHOUETTE *Romance*®

Published by Silhouette Books

America's Publisher of Contemporary Romance

SILHOUETTE BOOKS

ISBN 0-373-19686-5

TO KISS A SHEIK

Copyright © 2003 by Teresa Ann Southwick

All rights reserved. Except for use in any review, the reproduction
or utilization of this work in whole or in part in any form by any
electronic, mechanical or other means, now known or hereafter
invented, including xerography, photocopying and recording, or in
any information storage or retrieval system, is forbidden without
the written permission of the editorial office, Silhouette Books,
233 Broadway, New York, NY 10279 U.S.A.

All characters in this book have no existence outside the imagination of
the author and have no relation whatsoever to anyone bearing the same
name or names. They are not even distantly inspired by any individual
known or unknown to the author, and all incidents are pure invention.

This edition published by arrangement with Harlequin Books S.A.

® and TM are trademarks of Harlequin Books S.A., used under license.
Trademarks indicated with ® are registered in the United States Patent
and Trademark Office, the Canadian Trade Marks Office and in other
countries.

Visit Silhouette at www.eHarlequin.com

Printed in U.S.A.

Books by Teresa Southwick

Silhouette Romance

Wedding Rings and Baby Things #1209
The Bachelor's Baby #1233
*A Vow, a Ring, a Baby Swing #1349
The Way to a Cowboy's Heart #1383
*And Then He Kissed Me #1405
*With a Little T.L.C. #1421
The Acquired Bride #1474
*Secret Ingredient: Love #1495
*The Last Marchetti Bachelor #1513
**Crazy for Lovin' You #1529
**This Kiss #1541
**If You Don't Know by Now #1560
**What If We Fall in Love? #1572
Sky Full of Promise #1624
†To Catch a Sheik #1674
†To Kiss a Sheik #1686

Silhouette Books

The Fortunes of Texas
Shotgun Vows

Silhouette Special Edition

The Summer House #1510
  "Courting Cassandra"
*Midnight, Moonlight
  & Miracles* #1517

*The Marchetti Family
**Destiny, Texas
†Desert Brides

TERESA SOUTHWICK

lives in Southern California with her hero husband, who
is more than happy to share with her the male point of
view. An avid fan of romance novels, she is delighted to
be living out her dream of writing for Silhouette Books.

Teresa has also written historical romances under the
same name.

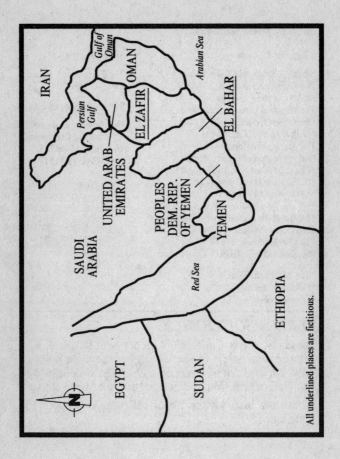

All underlined places are fictitious.

Chapter One

She felt like Clark Kent on a bad day.

Crystal Rawlins adjusted her large, ugly glasses making sure they covered as much of her face as possible. She wasn't used to this limitation to her peripheral vision, but it was necessary for her disguise. Now it was showtime.

"I'm Crystal Rawlins," she said to His Highness, Fariq Hassan, as they stood in his office, his polished, cherrywood desk beside them.

"Yes. The new nanny. Welcome to El Zafir, Miss Rawlins. I am pleased to meet you."

He was the flesh-and-blood definition of tall, dark and wow. He could be the model for the handsome prince in a fairy tale. Smiling politely, he extended his hand.

Shake hands with the devil.

The unwitting thought raced through her mind as Crystal put her palm in his much larger one. She had no idea if he *was* a devil. But she discovered that his elegant fingers were warm and strong as he applied firm pressure to her own. For some reason, she hadn't been prepared for his touch. The contact, although brief, sent her already fidgety nerves into a tap dance.

Normally when she reported for her first day on a job, she was wearing carefully applied makeup and an outfit that made her feel professional and confident. But this wasn't like any job she'd ever had in terms of circumstances, money or importance. And the stakes had never been so high before. In a twist of fate that defied logic, looking her best could get her fired. If that happened, who would pay her mother's medical bills? Creditors were threatening to take everything she owned—including the house Crystal had grown up in—and it wasn't going to happen on her watch.

"I am very pleased to meet you at last, Your Highness. I've done some research and discovered many wonderful things about your country. I'm grateful for the opportunity to work here."

He was studying her. "Even though the contract is for three years? Vacations aside, it is a long time to be away from your home."

"Job security is a good thing."

He nodded approvingly. "It is indeed. As is stability for my children."

"Your aunt said keeping the position filled has been a problem. Five nannies in a year, I believe?"

"Yes." He frowned.

"I assure you that I have every intention of fulfilling my contract."

"Good. I can see why my aunt spoke so highly of you after your meeting with her in New York."

"Princess Farrah has excellent taste—" She stopped. That sounded terribly egotistical, and not at all what she'd meant. "That is, the princess seemed a fastidious and perceptive woman with excellent taste in fashion."

"Also nannies, I hope."

"And nephews," she mumbled.

"Excuse me?"

She looked around, taking a moment to catch her breath before her nerves started to show. Until that slip, she thought she'd managed to sound calm and in control. It was an act to go along with the new look.

"I said 'and here.' What a nice place you've got."

"Thank you."

Fariq was the father of the five-year-old twins she'd been hired to look after. It was important to get off on the right foot—*and* the left foot. She'd expected first-day-on-the-job jitters, but not like this; he was disturbingly good-looking. But she'd always believed beauty was only skin deep. Character came from within. This was her chance to put her money where her mouth was.

She was face to face with her boss, who, if not the best-looking man she'd ever seen, was certainly in the top three, and all she had going for her was her naked face. What she wouldn't give for the crutch of cosmetics, or the props of high-heeled pumps and a tailored business suit.

Crystal was trying to pull off a plain appearance, as stated in the list of requirements for this position. That was a challenge for a former beauty queen, the pride and joy of her hometown, Pullman, Washington—population nine thousand when the university was in summer session. In that other life, success was all about appearance. This was the flip side of the coin—her moment of truth. Would the prince see past the hideous glasses, shapeless long-skirted navy suit, sturdy sensible shoes and hair pulled back from her face so tightly she looked like an ad for the facelift doctor *not* to use?

If he did, she would be sent packing, without the very generous salary that was the main reason she'd come here; the other reason being the opportunity to travel and experience life. That reason was important to her mother and had been the only way Crystal could get her to accept financial help.

"Please have a seat, Miss Rawlins." He held out his hand, indicating the chair in front of his desk.

"Thank you."

She sat and resisted the inclination to sigh in ecstasy at the soft, supple leather of the barrel-back chair.

"So," he said, rounding his desk, then sitting behind it. He met her gaze. "How was your trip from—" he looked down at what was probably her employment paperwork "—Washington? The home of delicious apples, I believe."

"Not in Pullman. It's wheat—all wheat all the time. And my trip was very long, Your Highness. I lost track of how many time zones I crossed."

"Yes."

Fariq Hassan was the middle of King Gamil's three sons and apparently didn't waste words. Her research on the fabulously wealthy royal family of this near-idyllic Middle-Eastern country revealed that they didn't keep an especially low social profile. His younger brother, Rafiq, was something of a playboy. The eldest son, Crown Prince Kamal, heir to the country's throne, was considered by the press to be the most eligible royal bachelor. And Fariq was a widower, sought after by some of the world's most beautiful jet-setting women.

No wonder. It had taken her all of ten seconds to research the fact that Fariq was probably the best-looking prince she'd ever laid eyes on. Not as flippant as it sounded since he was the *only* prince she'd ever laid eyes on. But she'd seen pictures of all three Hassan brothers in tabloids and magazines. They could be trouble in triplicate to female hearts.

In addition to his tall, powerful physique, number two sheik's black hair and smoldering good looks made it a real challenge to take her eyes off him. And Crystal took great satisfaction in her recently acquired skill of overlooking a handsome face. Just as Clark Kent was invulnerable to anything but Kryptonite, she was impervious to the charms of your average, ordinary, everyday, run-of-the-mill normal hunk. But Fariq Hassan was *so* not average, ordinary, everyday *or* normal.

"Are you recovered from your trip?" he asked politely.

"I'm getting there. Yesterday I felt like something the cat dragged in," she admitted. "I probably looked that way, too," she added, testing the waters.

"I'm sure that wasn't the case."

"You're very kind. And I'm grateful for the chance to acclimate. I very much appreciated the time to rest up in order to make a favorable impression on you and the children."

"Tell me about your experience with children."

He studied her carefully but his eyes gave no hint of anything besides normal curiosity. If anyone had learned to pick up a blip of masculine interest on her feminine radar it was Crystal. She'd had enough unwelcome practice and she'd made up her mind not to be arm candy ever again. His neutral reaction was a sign her masquerade was working. So why was she vaguely disappointed that he didn't find her the tiniest bit attractive?

"I paid my way through college with money I earned doing child care." And scholarship money for placing second in a local beauty pageant. "My degree is in elementary education. After graduation, I took a position for a year with a well-to-do family in Seattle. You probably have my letters of recommendation in front of you."

"Your references are impeccable. A degree in education?" he asked, meeting her gaze.

Those black eyes of his seemed to see right through her. Like X-ray vision. She might be a Clark Kent in training, but which one of them was *really* a super hero in disguise?

"Eventually I'd like to teach." She sat up as tall as she possibly could and pulled her shoulders back, meeting his gaze in what was her best I've-got-nothing-to-hide attitude.

"You have no desire for a family of your own?" One midnight-dark eyebrow lifted.

"Someday. But there are things I want to do before love, marriage and children."

"In that order?"

"What other order would there be?"

A corner of his mouth curved upward. "Children then marriage."

Her cheeks grew hot at the suggestion of bedding before wedding. That arrangement raised no eyebrows in this day and age and she didn't judge anyone else for it. But there was something about talking so intimately with this man that just made her burn all over.

She shifted in her leather chair, then met his gaze. "Your Highness, I'm not so naive that I don't know this happens. But not to me."

"I see. But don't American women pride themselves

on the ability to have a career and family at the same time? What is the point in waiting, Miss Rawlins?''

''Because that's not the way I want to do it. I adore children, which is why I chose a career in education. And when I have my own, I intend to stay home and raise them. But when the time is right, I'll go back to work. My teaching schedule will allow me to spend holidays and vacations with my children.''

''Ah. A planner. Very organized.'' He frowned.

''You disapprove?''

''On the contrary. I find the characteristic quite refreshing.''

He didn't look as if he found it refreshing. He looked as though he didn't believe her. She clasped her hands together and rested them in the her lap. ''May I ask you something?''

''Yes.''

''Forgive me if this sounds impertinent, but as an educator I've learned it's important to create an atmosphere where no question is perceived as stupid.''

His mouth turned up. ''I see. Now that you've qualified yourself, please, ask your stupid question.''

She wasn't quite sure if he was laughing at her or not. But she decided not to let it put her off. She was who she was, and because of his children, they would be dealing with each other. It was important for him to be clear on the fact that she was a woman who spoke her mind.

''It's not actually a stupid question. It's along the lines of a stupid clarification. This…talk we're having feels more like an interview than a meet-and-greet.''

''Excuse me?''

''You know—we introduce ourselves and you welcome me to your country. Which you've done quite nicely. But I was under the impression that I'd already been hired for the position."

He nodded. "Aunt Farrah was most impressed with you, and I respect her opinion very much. But these are *my* children, Miss Rawlins. The final decision is mine."

"So if you disagree with Princess Farrah—"

"You will be on the first plane back to the United States," he stated bluntly.

"Which brings up another question."

"A stupid one?" He flashed a grin taking any sting— perceived or otherwise—from the words.

"I...I hope not." She cleared her throat. "Why did you require an American nanny? Why not a woman from your own country, familiar with El Zafirian customs?"

"I will teach my children about their country. As will the rest of my family. But many of our business dealings are in the West, and, by virtue of their birth, Hana and Nuri will be involved in service to El Zafir. They will be required to interact with representatives of America. You will be able to prepare them for this, which someone from my country could not. It is a requirement I think very important."

She swallowed. "About the position's qualifications, Your Highness."

"They were not plain enough?"

"Interesting you phrased it that way. May I ask why a *plain* woman is required?"

"Actually I believe the phrasing was 'a plain, unobtrusive American woman with some intelligence, who is good with children.'"

Crystal figured she could be as unobtrusive as the next woman and it had taken a reasonable degree of smarts for her to get through college. She was the youngest of five children, and all of her older siblings had kids she adored. The "good with children" part she wasn't worried about. It was the "plain" part that puzzled her.

For fun she'd looked up the definition which ranged from discreet and simple to ugly and unattractive. Did he realize that she could be insulted by the phrasing? Mostly she was curious.

"I understand the significance of the rest. But your aunt didn't explain why 'plain' is important."

"Because beautiful women are…" He hesitated and his eyes turned hard—icy and hot at the same time. His mouth thinned to a straight line.

"Are what?" she asked, shivering at the expression on his face.

"An unwelcome distraction."

"I see."

She'd expected arrogance. She'd prepared herself for arrogance. She hadn't been disappointed. Still, until she'd brought up the current subject, his royal arrogance had exuded a warmth and politeness that she found disarming and completely charming. His sudden coolness told her he had a story, and it wouldn't surprise her if a beautiful woman was involved. She was curious to know what had happened to him. And she might just be here long enough to find out—if he didn't see through her disguise and send her packing.

Then his comment really sank in and pushed her buttons. *Beautiful women* an unwelcome distraction? It was no fault of *his* if he became distracted? A knot of annoyance tightened inside her. Apparently there was no way to adequately prepare for his brand of arrogance. She was raised to take responsibility for her actions, but maybe a sheik could get away with blaming others for his flaws.

"Your Highness," she began. "Let me make sure I understand. If *you* are unable to stay on task, as we say in the education field, it is the fault of the woman—if she happens to be beautiful?"

Again she lifted her chin and met his gaze straight on, letting him get a good look at her. If her disguise couldn't hold up under scrutiny, it was best to know now. She'd considered a wig, buck teeth and a fake wart on her nose. In this situation, she felt simplicity was the cornerstone of success. Yet she'd always been unable to suspend her disbelief when no one could tell that Clark Kent was who he really was—merely because he slicked down his hair and wore unappealing glasses. There was still that mouthwatering body. A hunk by any other name... Right?

She didn't consider herself beautiful—not in the leagues Prince Fariq Hassan played in. But back home she'd had her share of attention, not all positive. She had the scars to prove it. She didn't think her looks, or lack thereof, should be the basis for whether or not she was qualified to care for his children.

They stared at each other for several moments, and she wished he would say something. She figured this was where her mouth had yet again written a check her cockiness couldn't cash. Still, it was better to know now—for both of them. And especially for the children.

"Let me see if *I* understand the question," he said. There was a gleam in his eyes that *could* be humor. "If I am unable to concentrate in the presence of a beautiful woman you are asking who's to blame?"

"That about sums it up."

"It's her fault, of course."

Again she didn't know whether or not he was joking and decided to behave as if he wasn't. "Then there's something you need to know about me before we go any further."

He folded his hands together, then placed them on his desk as he leaned forward. "What is that?"

"The foundation of my philosophy in dealing with children is that one always needs to take responsibility for one's actions."

"And there's something you should know about me."

"What is that?"

"I'm not a child. And I'm never wrong."

He was so inherently masculine in such a very primal way that his first statement bordered on ludicrous. "Duh" was her instinctive mental response and nearly distracted her from the swagger in his second statement. Never wrong?

"It's always good to know where your employer stands on an issue," she said. "Assuming you still are my employer. Or that I'm your employee." She held her breath.

"I think my aunt has chosen well. You'll do nicely."

Crystal realized she should have been elated that she'd passed muster. She was in. Hired. She'd cleared the hurdle. Before meeting the prince it was what she'd hoped to do. Unfortunately, now that her job was in the bag, she felt oddly deflated at her rousing success. He believed she was as plain as she pretended. How about them apples?

Most people associated all of Washington state with apples. Even Fariq had. Which just goes to show you should never assume anything. But he took her clothes, hair and glasses at face value and looked no further.

She sighed. Oddly enough, she felt that life could be compared to an apple—at its core. You could always count on the fact that there were seeds to spit or swallow and Fariq was hers. And yet she had to respect the man. In spite of a thumbs-up from a trusted family member and the fact that people in his position paid others to raise their children, he loved his kids so much he'd insisted on meeting her. It was obviously important to him to see for himself and approve of the person who would care for them.

"I'm very anxious to meet the children," she said. If this were an interview, she would be guilty of leading it. But technically it wasn't. And she *was* eager to meet her charges.

"I will take you to them and introduce you." There was a note of pride in his voice and a tender look in his eyes.

He stood and rounded the desk, then held out his arm indicating she should precede him. She stopped at the heavy wooden door. At the same time they both reached out to open it, and their hands touched.

"Allow me," he said. His butterscotch-and-brandy voice made her shiver.

"Thank you."

In the hall outside his office, she looked around. Her low-heeled shoes sank into the thick, plush carpet. Wood paneling lined walls hung with ornately framed enhanced photos of El Zafir in various stages of development.

In all her life she'd never seen such luxury as she had since arriving at the palace. Marble floors, grand staircases, a fountain in the foyer, lush gardens. There were sinfully expensive furnishings and gold fixtures everywhere—priceless art, paintings, vases and tapestries, oh, my.

And big. The number of rooms in this place would give an army of Molly Maids a lifetime of job security. Not to mention a girl could walk off a whole lot of chocolate indulgence here. "Wow" didn't do justice to her feelings, but it was the first word that kept coming to mind.

When she'd arrived in the business wing for her meeting with the prince, her nerves had obscured her surroundings. Now that she'd passed the first hurdle, she noticed a lot more. There were four offices. The king's was first, then the crown prince, followed by Fariq's, where she now stood. To her right at the end of the hall was the last one, and she guessed it belonged to Rafiq, the youngest of the brothers. She thought she heard children's voices, then shrieks of laughter.

Glancing up—way up—at her employer and guide, she cocked her thumb in the direction of the noise and said, "They went thataway."

"A reference to the B-Westerns of your country," he commented.

"You know the expression."

"I attended college and graduate school in America."

"Of course. I knew that."

They turned into the last office and there on the leather sofa against the wall sat two children and a man who could only be Fariq's brother. A little girl sat on one knee and was messing up his hair. At the same time Prince Rafiq was tickling the boy who occupied his other knee, the child shrieking with laughter at the same time he begged him to stop. No doubt these were the five-year-old twins who would be in her care.

"And they say men are incapable of multitasking," Crystal couldn't resist saying.

Fariq lifted one eyebrow. "Guard the secret well."

The gleam in his eyes and the smile curving his lips told her he was teasing and capable of humor. She wasn't quite sure what to do with the information and didn't have a chance to figure it out. Suddenly the boy and girl squealed.

"Papa!" the children said at the same time.

They jumped off the couch and ran to him, each wrapping their arms around one of his long legs. He bent at the waist and embraced them.

"Hello, little one," he said, running a knuckle tenderly down his daughter's nose. She looked up at him adoringly. "And you." He grinned at his son as he ruffled the boy's hair. "There's someone here who wants to meet you," he said. Suddenly two pairs of very dark, very curious and just a bit shy eyes were turned on her. "This is Miss Rawlins. What do you say?"

"Hi," the boy glanced up at his father. "I mean how do you do?"

Fariq nodded approvingly.

The little girl still clutched his leg. "How do you do?" she mimicked her brother.

The prince smiled tenderly at his daughter then angled his chin toward the other man. "That poor excuse for a nanny is my younger brother Rafiq."

"Your Highness," she said, acknowledging the adult introduction first.

The prince stood and ran his hands through his disheveled hair, attempting to correct the damage his niece had inflicted. Any man who would play with children at the expense of his appearance was all right in her book.

"It's a pleasure to meet you, Miss Rawlins," he said, extending his hand.

"And you, Your—"

"Call me Rafiq. I insist," he said before she could protest.

"Thank you." She looked first at the boy, then his sister. "This must be Nuri and Hana."

"How did you know our names?" the little girl asked, clearly impressed. She blinked huge, beautiful black eyes fringed by exceptionally long thick lashes.

In fifteen years, probably less, the male population of El Zafir had better hang on to their hearts with both hands, Crystal thought. "Your Aunt Farrah told me. When I met her in New York, she showed me pictures of you both."

"Your glasses are very large," Nuri said. "And very ugly." He was as handsome as his sister was beautiful and had no doubt picked up a dash of arrogance from his father.

"You're very observant," she said dryly.

"Your hair is too tight," Hana said.

"It only looks that way," Crystal answered quickly. But the beginnings of a headache put a lie to her words.

"Does it hurt?" Hana asked, studying her intently.

"No." Crystal looked from one tall man to the other, then fixed a gaze on the children's father. "May I ask a question, Your—"

"Fariq," he said. "My brother is correct. There's no need for formality in private. And I will call you Crystal."

"All right. Fariq." She tested the name and found she very much liked the exotic sound.

"Is it a stupid question?" he asked, with a look she now knew meant he was joking.

"You're going to make me regret that remark, aren't you?" she said, smiling. "Never mind. I'll risk it. I was just wondering if you take the children to work with you often."

"You mean because they are here with my brother," he stated. "The answer to that question is no. But my little brother offered to pick up the slack, as you Americans say. Because he blames himself for the last nanny's sudden and less-than-dignified departure."

"It wasn't my fault," the other man protested, a twinkle in his eyes.

"Don't fib, uncle," Nuri said. "Nanny was in your bed."

"How do you know that?" The stern facade was destroyed by his half smile.

"Aunt Farrah told grandfather," the boy explained. "Then he said the new one must be a dried-up old prune."

"How did you hear that?" Fariq's tone was disapproving.

"Nuri was hiding behind Aunt Farrah's sofa again," Hana cheerfully volunteered. She looked shyly at Crystal. "I'm *glad* you're not old or dried up."

"That goes double for me," Crystal said, grateful that someone in the royal family could see the forest for the trees.

"Little one, you shouldn't tattle on your brother," the prince admonished his daughter.

"Even if it's the truth and he's naughty?" the girl wanted to know.

"Even so," he explained. "Family loyalty is a treasure."

Fariq enjoyed the embarrassed exasperation clearly visible on his brother's face and struggled not to laugh at his son's words. He'd been unaware that the boy knew details of the former nanny's downfall, but it was the truth. A word to the wise would be in order, he thought, watching Crystal carefully observing his brother. He wondered what she was thinking.

Fariq cleared his throat. "Like every woman Rafiq meets, the former nanny developed a crush on him. Her actions were an effort to garner his regard. The resulting attention was probably not what she'd had in mind."

Crystal's eyes widened. "I think I can guess what that attention was since I'm here and she's not."

"Instant dismissal," Rafiq confirmed. "I talked the king out of beheading her."

Hana giggled. "You're fibbing again, Uncle."

"Yes, little one. Your uncle is quite the fibber," Fariq agreed. "He claims to have rebuffed her advances."

"It is the truth," he protested. "Innocently, I walked into my room and there she was. I immediately turned and walked out again. Father believed me."

"The king was uninterested in explanations," Fariq said to Crystal. "He ordered my brother to cease and desist flirting with the staff and to find a wife and settle down. His exact words were that he didn't want justice, merely peace and quiet."

"I can understand why," she answered.

"But there was still the matter of no nanny." And the necessity of finding another. Since the twins' own mother was gone. That thought was followed by a familiar twist of anger. The woman still had the power to arouse his ire, further stoking his displeasure.

Fariq looked at his new nanny. "I was in negotiations to bring a hotel and a well-known, upscale department store to El Zafir. It was decided that Aunt Farrah would go to the world-renown employment agency in New York.''

Fariq hadn't disagreed with his father's stipulation. In fact, he'd thought the addition to the list of qualifications a good idea. He had no wish to deal with a woman hiding a duplicitous heart by flaunting the face of an angel. Once had been enough.

He decided Crystal was exactly what the king had in mind when he'd made his decree. And his children had a keen eye for detail, he thought proudly. Her glasses were indeed very large and ugly, but they couldn't quite hide her engaging, hazel eyes. Cat's eyes. They shimmered with intelligence and humor. He'd seen through her spectacles, although they did conceal a good deal of the upper half of her face. Still, the skin he *could* see was flawless and smooth.

Her hair was brown, and the severe style hid any possible attractive shadings. It did look quite painful. He wouldn't be surprised if her eyebrows behind the glasses had a permanent, quizzical arch to them. But he couldn't fault her for having a single strand of hair out of place.

Her loose-fitting navy skirt skimmed her ankles and was topped by a matching jacket that he couldn't help wishing was a bit shorter and more tailored—so that he might get a better idea of her shape. The ankles he *could* see showed great potential for the rest of her legs hidden from his view. And he was a bit curious about the exact contour of the limbs attached to the ankles with such potential. But curiosity killed the cat, he reminded himself. Therefore he should be grateful for the conservative attire that restricted his view. Because he needed a nanny, and his aunt had assured him Crystal was perfect.

He had to agree. He liked her forthright manner. Lack of pretense was a character trait he'd learned to value the hard way. Crystal said what she was thinking. It was most refreshing.

Then there was the sense of humor she'd revealed in their conversation. It was evidence of a lively and quick mind. He found he liked her and the thought raised a warning. Which he chose to overlook. It merely meant that their interaction regarding the children would be more efficient. If those encounters had the potential to be the slightest bit entertaining, he would merely ignore any pleasurable sensations.

He agreed with his aunt. She seemed perfect. Except for one small thing—her smile. He'd seen it a few minutes ago when her lips had curved upward revealing straight, white teeth, and he'd found the expression quite lovely.

When Crystal smiled again, this time a tender look for his daughter, Fariq felt an odd sensation in his chest. He attempted to disregard it as he listened to her soft, clear, melodic voice. She exuded warmth and a nurturing spirit. Something important for the children. Nothing else mattered.

Crystal bent to look directly at the child. "Hana, I agree with your father about tattling. But I also remember how good it feels to get something on your brother."

"You have a brother, Crystal?" Rafiq asked.

"Four," she clarified, straightening. "I'm the youngest. And I'm ashamed to admit I was a bit of a tattler in my day."

Fariq looked at her. "How did your brothers deal with that?"

"Not well. But there wasn't much they could do after

my dad ordered them not to lay a hand on me. 'You don't hit girls,' he always said.''

"A man who would strike a woman is swine," Rafiq agreed.

"According to my father he's worse than the stuff cleaned out of swine cages," she said.

"Your father is undoubtedly an honorable man." Which boded well for his raising an honorable daughter. Fariq met her gaze. "My country has no tolerance for abusers of women. The transgression is dealt with severely."

"As are lies and deceit," Rafiq interjected self-righteously.

Fariq caught a look on Crystal's face and thought her lovely skin paled. He looked at his brother and asked, "What are you talking about?"

"Your lies and deceit have corrupted my good name. I am an honorable man who speaks only the truth. I do not know why our father holds me responsible for that woman's reprehensible behavior. It's *not* my fault."

"What was it Shakespeare said about protesting too much?" Fariq asked.

But maybe his brother couldn't help it that women found him charming. It was easy if one had never been deceived and played for a fool. When that happened, a wise man went out of his way *not* to attract attention from the opposite sex.

Rafiq looked at Crystal. "Do you think I'm the kind of man who would be dishonest?"

"I hardly know you," she answered. Then she blinked and her eyes widened. "What I meant to say is—"

"Never mind," Fariq interrupted. "No need to sugarcoat it as you Americans say. Your first answer was accurate.''

"So get to know me," Rafiq invited. "At dinner tonight. The whole family will be there. Decide for yourself."

Here he goes again, Fariq thought. Ever the charmer. But for some reason, his brother's attentiveness toward Crystal bothered him. Was it her artless remark about the order of love, marriage and children? Damn him. She was far too innocent to deal with Rafiq's flirtations.

"Yes, please," Hana said, putting her hands together in a gesture of supplication directed at Crystal.

Fariq knew his daughter. The little girl who didn't usually trust easily had taken to this woman right away. "My brother is correct. You must meet the family. Dinner is at seven."

"Very well. Thank you."

She said the correct words easily. But Fariq wondered why his newest employee looked more as if she'd been sentenced to a beheading in the Casbah square. He would make it a point to find out.

Chapter Two

Four hours ago Crystal had left the palace business wing pale as a ghost after receiving an invitation from her boss to dine with the *entire* royal family. Now she was sitting at their table wondering if any color had returned to her face. Even the fact that she was eminently qualified for the nanny position didn't make her feel better about taking her ruse out for a test drive in front of the entire family. For goodness' sake, Rafiq had joked about beheading the last nanny. He'd looked as if he was kidding, but many a truth was spoken in jest.

"I believe the new nanny is a fraud." Princess Farrah studied her.

Crystal froze. Heart pounding, she ceased and desisted rubbing the gold edge on her china dinner plate and felt that if any color had returned to her cheeks, it had just drained away again. She forced herself to meet the princess' gaze. "Excuse me?"

"You're quiet—not at all the vivacious young woman you were when we met in New York."

Okay. Royal humor through exaggeration. She tucked the info away. "According to my mother it's always better to not say anything and risk being thought simpleminded than to open your mouth and prove it."

"A wise woman, your mother," King Gamil commented.

"Yes, she is."

Crystal glanced to her left toward the head of the table where the king sat watching her. She guessed his age to be somewhere in his mid to late fifties. He was still quite handsome, and the silver glistening at his temples also streaked his black hair, giving a distinguished air to his good looks. Her mother would have said he worked for her in a big way.

Vicki Rawlins would have loved dining with the royal family of El Zafir. Married and a mother before saying goodbye to her teens, she'd frequently vocalized her regrets at never experiencing life outside of Pullman, Washington. After Crystal graduated from college, her parents had finally been in a position to do the traveling her mother had always longed for. But that wasn't to be. They'd divorced, shocking everyone. Then there'd been her mother's devastating car accident, followed by a slow, painful and expensive recovery.

In spite of that, or maybe because of it, she'd encouraged her youngest child and only daughter to do everything she wanted before settling down with a husband and starting a family. She'd been giddy with excitement when she'd learned about Crystal snagging this job. That and the generous salary were the reasons Crystal was so determined to make this employment experience a success. Failure was not an option. She'd rather be beheaded.

"The fact you are so quiet," the king continued,

"does this mean you are not enjoying yourself this evening?"

"On the contrary, Your Majesty. I've never had such a wonderful dinner."

It was being scrutinized by the entire royal family that had her nervous as a long-tailed cat in a roomful of rocking chairs.

"I'm glad you are enjoying the food." The king set down his gold fork.

"And the company is exemplary, too," she said.

Glancing around the table, she noted that the king's sons had inherited superior DNA, probably from their good-looking and distinguished father. During the cocktail hour before dinner, she had finally met Crown Prince Kamal, the third of the three princes. Like his brothers, he was tall, dark and devilishly handsome. Although, in her humble opinion, Fariq was by far the best looking. But anyone could see the royal family of El Zafir was extremely photogenic, which was no doubt one of the reasons they frequently appeared in the tabloids.

Princess Farrah was the king's sister and seemed to fill the family post of feminine guiding hand for the widower. Her age was impossible to guess. She could be anywhere from forty to sixty, although Crystal leaned toward the low end. The woman looked fabulous with her dark hair stylishly cut into a sleek style that barely brushed the collar of her royal-blue Chanel suit. Her black eyes appeared huge with the assistance of subtle cosmetics.

Princess Johara, the king's youngest child and only daughter, was seventeen. She was a strikingly lovely girl with large black eyes and a delicate look. She sat on the same side of the table with Crystal. Hana was between them with Nuri on the teen's other side.

"I can't help feeling there's another reason for your restraint," Fariq commented. "Something other than caution."

"Really?" she said, stalling. The man was far too perceptive for her own good.

"Is it possible that you are intimidated by your surroundings?" he asked.

"Me? Intimidated?"

She was a small-town girl from eastern Washington. Tonight her surroundings included the entire royal family of an oil-rich country swiftly emerging onto the world stage. She was in a large room filled with the most expensive furnishings she'd ever seen. Candles flickered in crystal wall sconces, and fragrant flowers graced the dining table, as well as numerous arrangements artfully placed on occasional tables. The cloth covering the dining table probably cost more than she could earn in a month. It would be just her luck to spill something on it in front of the entire royal family and stain the sucker so badly even homemaker high priestess Martha Stewart would have no removal remedy.

Hysterical laughter threatened. Crystal managed to hold it back as she glanced around the table, a surface so long and flat it made her wonder if the royal pilot could land the royal jet on it. She wasn't a country bumpkin by any means, but these surroundings *were* intimidating. Her frame of reference lacked anything on this scale.

For goodness' sake, the china was edged in gold, the real, honest-to-goodness, solid twenty-four karat variety. Intimidated? She felt like a sumo wrestler in a tearoom.

"Now that you mention it," she said meeting Fariq's amused gaze, "I am a tad overwhelmed by my surroundings."

"Please don't be," Princess Farrah said. "We're just normal people."

"Define *normal*." Crystal laughed. "Your Highness, My family has never had a cocktail hour before dinner and formal dress is T-shirt, jeans and sneakers."

She glanced down at her plain, unflattering drab brown dress and sighed. Even if she'd known after-five attire was required for the job, she couldn't have worn anything that flattered her. Beside her, Hana slid from her chair and ducked beneath the table to retrieve the napkin that had slipped off her lap.

The king frowned as he cleared his throat. "Perhaps we are a bit more formal that the average family. But I join with Farrah in urging you to relax and be yourself. May I say my sister did an admirable job in hiring you. I think you'll make a splendid nanny for Nuri. And perhaps Hana if she comes out from beneath the table," he said disapprovingly.

The little girl put a hand over her mouth to stifle a giggle as she looked up at Crystal. She wished she'd already assumed her full duties so she could rescue these restless children and get them ready for bed. But she wasn't to take over until tomorrow. At least the two five-year-olds were still in good spirits. If that changed, she would have to say something. After winking at the little girl, she patted the chair beside her and the child scrambled into it.

"Thank you, Your Majesty. I appreciate your endorsement." She smiled at him and let out a breath.

Her adrenaline was beginning to settle after spiking off the scale from the "fraud" remark. So far, so good.

No one had seen past the ugly glasses and tasteless clothes. She should be grateful. She should be exhilarated. She should be doing the dance of joy. But she wasn't. And that confused her.

"May I inquire where you went to school?" Kamal asked. He was more serious than his brothers. Rafiq was friendly and charming. Fariq was sedate, although he'd revealed the humor lurking behind his reserved exterior. But she had yet to see Kamal crack a smile.

"I went to the University of Washington."

"What did you study?" he asked.

"I majored in elementary education with a minor in childhood behavior."

"What other attributes qualify you to look after my niece and nephew?" he asked.

She glanced at Fariq and was sure there was the hint of amusement in his gaze. Here we go again, she thought. It felt like yet another interview. This was the third time. Dare she hope it was the charm?

"I worked my way through college taking care of children for well-to-do families during summer and winter breaks. I believe my references are included with the résumé I gave Princess Farrah."

"I will look them over," Kamal said.

Crystal wondered if these people ever communicated with each other or simply repeated everything because they were conscientious overachievers. She couldn't resist a question of her own as she gazed around the table. "Is there anyone else who wants to interview me and make certain I'm qualified?" she asked sweetly.

Princess Farrah waved her hand in dismissal. "Don't let the Hassan men frighten you, my dear. You had the position when I hired you in New York. My nephews merely have a penchant for posturing."

Fariq put down his crystal water glass. "It is not posturing to be thorough when it comes to my children."

"I agree. And the children are very dear to me, as well," Farrah maintained. "The New York agency has a reputation for being the best. With their help, I conducted a meticulous and painstaking search for the perfect nanny. Hana and Nuri will be in excellent hands. Crystal is an admirable young woman."

"Time will tell," he said.

Crystal thought Fariq's words and especially the cynical expression on his face contained hidden challenges. Before she could decide whether or not she should worry, Nuri slid under the table after his napkin.

Johara didn't notice. She stared at her father. "I want to go to New York."

"It's just a city," her father commented, dismissing her comment. "You are far better off here. It is your home and where you belong."

"I don't want to be safe. I don't want to belong. I want to have experiences. I wish to live my life without everyone telling me—"

The king waved his hand impatiently. "Nonsense, Johara. It is time you let go of your foolish dreams."

"They're not foolish dreams—"

"Enough," the king said. "I do not wish to hear more of your girlish fantasies. Speak of it no more."

The young woman shot a dark look in his direction. She obeyed his command to keep silent but hostility radiated from her in nearly tangible waves. And Crystal couldn't blame her.

She knew the king was heralded as a monarch who listened to his people's needs and heeded them as best he could. But if he didn't start listening and heeding under his own roof, there would be hell to pay. El Zafir might be located on the other side of the world from the United States, but she would bet its teenagers shared the same wants, needs and characteristics. One of which was the yearning to be validated and taken seriously, not to mention pursuing happiness…and rebellion in the quest for independence.

"So tell me, Crystal, do you have a political affiliation in your country?" the king asked, completely changing the subject.

Although she wanted to shake him and tell him to ask his daughter what her beliefs were, she held back. In fact, after being grilled like an expensive steak by the male members of the royal family, she was beginning to wish they would treat her more like the teenage princess and ignore her completely.

She met the king's gaze. "Yes, Your Majesty. I'm a Republicrat."

There was sudden silence around the table, and she felt six pairs of eyes on her. It would have been eight, but the twins were squirming in their chairs and putting their napkins on their heads. They'd lost interest in the conversation right after the entree had been served. It was just a matter of time until they disappeared under the table together.

"Republicrat?" Fariq frowned. "I studied the politics of your country, but I have never heard of this party."

"Neither has anyone else. It has a membership of one. Basically I take the best from the Democrats and Republicans, then vote my conscience."

"Ah," he said, nodding. "You are a hybrid."

Mongrel, mixture, mutt. That described her to a T. "Exactly," she said, nodding emphatically.

"Crossbreeding in politics." The king nodded approvingly. "Shows responsibility as well as intelligence. You do not simply follow like a sheep. A woman who can think for herself."

"That's me," she agreed. "Crossbred in politics and ancestry. Nothing pedigreed about me."

"Thank goodness," Rafiq interjected, his expression serious. "I have much experience with horses, and it is my opinion that Thoroughbreds are a great deal of trouble."

"I'll let you know," she muttered, wondering what it would be like working with Fariq, whose bloodlines were probably impeccable.

"Excuse me?" he said, his gaze piercing as he met hers.

Thinking fast, she answered, "I said, I'll bet you know. Since your brother is an accomplished horseman, he would have firsthand knowledge of how much trouble purebreds are."

"Yes." Fariq sipped his champagne. "And people are much like horses in that regard."

Crystal's cheeks and neck grew hot. Was it possible he'd heard her mumbled words? Had he actually understood she'd been referring to the fact that his royal bloodlines could make him a pain in the neck?

"I'm not sure I follow you," she said.

"Thoroughbreds can be difficult and demanding. Not unlike my own children. I require someone of intelligence, strength and quality to guide them. One thing we have not discussed is your views on raising children."

Thank goodness they were leaving the subject of horses behind. She felt confident and qualified to discuss her views on child rearing. "I would be happy to review my philosophy whenever you'd like."

"What about now?" he asked, glancing around the table.

"Fine. It will save time since everyone is here. What would you like to know?"

"What are your views on discipline?" Fariq set his fine linen napkin beside his plate.

"I'm in favor of it, but I think any punishment should fit the crime."

At that moment little Hana hit her plate with her elbow, bumping it into her glass, which fell over with a crash. Water went everywhere and the goblet shattered.

"Oh, Nanny," the little girl said, hiding her face against Crystal's shoulder.

She put her arm around the child. "Don't worry, sweetie. Accidents happen."

"Johara," the king said sternly. He flashed the teenager an angry look as a server rushed forward to clean up the mess. "The children are your responsibility tonight. Make them behave."

"But, Father, they have been sitting too long—"

With one hand he waved away her excuse. "Take them to their rooms at once."

"With pleasure." The princess threw her napkin on the table and stood. "Hana, Nuri, come with me."

Crystal gave the little girl a quick hug before letting her go with her teenage aunt. When they were gone, an awkward silence filled the room.

Fariq cleared his throat. "And what punishment would you allot for that crime?"

"First of all that wasn't a crime, but an accident. If she'd done it on purpose that would be a different story." She glanced at the king, debating how blunt to be, then decided the whole royal kit and caboodle of them might as well know how she felt. "Second, I agree with Princess Johara. Five-year-olds have approximately forty-five minutes of model behavior in them. Hana and Nuri passed that three quarters of an hour ago. In my opinion they were way past their grace period. They *had* been sitting too long and needed their space, to be children.''

''What would you have done?'' Fariq asked, his expression unreadable.

''I'd have taken them back to their rooms and started the bedtime routine long ago.''

''But they are part of the royal family,'' the king protested.

''*Children* of the royal family,'' she stressed. ''Not just short adults. As they mature, they'll be able to handle the demands of pomp and circumstance. But they're only five, hardly more than babies.''

''But Johara—''

''Forgive me, Your Majesty,'' she interrupted. ''The princess is not to blame. Trying to control unpredictable five-year-olds would be like trying to harness the wind.''

''Crystal, you are so right.'' Princess Farrah delicately wiped her mouth with a napkin, then set it beside her plate. ''I plead ignorance in the art of child rearing, as I have none of my own. Gamil is hardly an expert, since all four of his offspring were raised by nannies and in boarding schools. I knew you would be perfect as soon as I met you.''

Crystal was grateful to the princess as she looked around the table and watched all the royal men mulling over her words and nodding in agreement. A bubble of satisfaction, liberally laced with exhilaration, expanded inside her.

Usually her appearance was what got her noticed. In

fact, she'd come way too close to marrying a man who'd decided she would make the perfect accessory wife for an attorney on the way up the ladder of success. He'd actually told her to keep her thoughts to herself, stand up straight with her chest out and look beautiful. She'd told him to stick his proposal in his ear.

It was refreshing to be taken seriously for her brains. In this job her looks were actually a handicap to overcome. But the shiver of excitement that raced down her spine when she found Fariq's hooded gaze on her made her wish for a little lipstick, mascara and a flattering dress. Unfortunately, she couldn't have it both ways. Until she'd been there a while and convinced him she was the best person to care for his children, she was forced to keep the secret.

"I appreciate that, Your Highness," she said to the princess as an ear-to-ear grin threatened. She managed to hold it back.

"Why is it you have no children of your own?" the princess asked her.

Fariq's eyes gleamed, making her think what a rascal he must have been as a boy. But he was a man and it made him look roguish, masculine and so exciting. That doggone shiver boogied up and down her spine again.

"Miss Rawlins believes in love, marriage and children. In that order," he added.

"Ah," the princess said, nodding. "And you have not met a man who makes your heart beat faster? Someone who turns your thoughts to love?"

Against her will, Crystal's gaze strayed to Fariq. Quickly she averted her eyes and looked at the king's sister. "No, Your Majesty. I was almost engaged once. But—"

"Almost?" Fariq asked. "And now?"

"He's out of my life," she said with a shrug. She was beginning to feel like the key player in the Spanish inquisition.

"So to turn your thoughts from a broken heart you accepted this position far from home?" Kamal asked.

She refused to address the broken-heart portion of the question. "From the time I was a little girl, my mother drilled it into me that it's best to experience life before you have responsibilities tying you down."

"Drilled? Interesting choice of words," Fariq commented.

"I have four brothers who followed my parents' example and married young, then started families right away. I'm the only one who hasn't and my mother's last hope to do as she said not as she did. I'm hoping to make her proud."

The first man to tempt her into overlooking her mother's tenet had only been interested in her as a tool to advance his career. There wouldn't be a second temptation. That game needed two players. Without warning, her thoughts fixed on Fariq. Silly. Because he wasn't likely to participate. Especially with a plain woman.

"So your mother's advice is our gain," Fariq commented.

"I hope you continue to feel that way." She removed her glasses for a moment and rubbed just above the bridge of her nose where the eye pads chafed. She missed her contacts—

Princess Farrah leaned toward her. "Crystal, do you really need your glasses to correct your vision?"

The question stunned her. Just when she'd thought it was safe to let her guard down, there was an unexpected zinger. Hurriedly she put her glasses back on and nearly poked herself in the eye.

"Why d-do you ask?"

"Because your eyes are quite lovely. And your skin is absolutely flawless—from what I can tell you aren't wearing cosmetics of any kind."

"I'm not." She sighed, deciding to leave it at that. "I'm blind as a bat without corrective lenses. Near sightedness combined with astigmatism distorts my vision terribly." At least that much was the honest truth. "Without my glasses I wouldn't be able to see across the table." She met Fariq's penetrating gaze and decided maybe that wouldn't be so bad. "Although in my own defense I'd like to point out it's quite a large table."

"Yes it is," the princess answered. "But how unfortunate. Without such eyewear, I believe you have the potential to be quite pretty. Have you ever considered looking into contacts?"

Crystal grinned. "Good one, Your Highness."

"What?" The woman's brow furrowed as she thought.

"Your pun—looking into contacts—"

"What does it matter?" Fariq's voice was edged with annoyance. "She's fine as she is. Beauty is a highly overrated quality."

Rafiq leaned his forearms against the table. "So, my brother, you would prefer a woman with a face that would stop a clock?"

"I didn't say that—"

"If beauty does not move you, what female attributes do you find enticing?" Kamal asked, the corners of his mouth curving up slightly.

"Honesty," Fariq said without hesitation.

Of all the attributes he could have named, that was the one Crystal could have done without. Not only that, this man had a high profile all over the world. His name had been linked with some of the world's most stunning women. But he was more interested in candor than comeliness. That pretty much shocked her right out of her support stockings.

So she said the only thing she could think of. "My mother always says beauty is as beauty does."

After several moments of silence the king asked, "What does that mean?"

"I'm not sure." Crystal shook her head. "I think it has something to do with using genetic gifts only for good."

Everyone laughed, including Fariq, and she was glad to have lightened a moment quickly becoming awkward and tense. With luck, Princess Farrah would stop trying to make her over. And what was that all about anyhow? What about the whole "plain" nanny scenario? It didn't take a billboard ad on the interstate for her to get the message that the king frowned on his sons pursuing anything of a personal nature with the hired help.

Crystal finally chalked it up to a chick thing. Women couldn't resist make-overs. She could only hope the matter would be dropped. Because she wasn't a super-hero. She had no tricks up her cape to preserve her alter ego. And she didn't want to think about what would happen if Fariq found out she could look better if she wanted.

Chapter Three

Fariq tossed the file he'd been reading onto the coffee table in his suite. The more he tried to concentrate on work, the more his thoughts turned to his children's new nanny. At dinner several hours before, he'd found her to be a curious yet intriguing mixture of spirit and intelligence.

He had sworn on the honor of his ancestors not to be taken in by a beautiful face ever again. Was it breaking his promise to think about this woman? She was certainly not the stunning sort with whom he was constantly and erroneously linked. But he'd found her pleasant and surprising.

He looked at the open French doors leading onto the balcony as a noise from outside drifted to him. After rising from the sofa, he walked to the doorway and glanced out. The night was dark as clouds covered the moon. But in the shadows to his right, he saw a figure leaning on the balcony railing outside the rooms where his children slept.

"Hello," he said.

Crystal whirled at the sound of his voice. Dim light from inside the suite illuminated her as she pressed a hand to her chest. "Good grief," she gasped, "I thought I was alone."

"And so you were until I came outside. This balcony runs the length of my suite. All the rooms are connected by it, and from here we can see the ocean. My bedroom is there," he said pointing to the room past the living area.

"Oh. I didn't actually understand the layout. I just came out for some air. I'm sorry if I disturbed you."

"You didn't," he lied.

She'd disturbed him even before he'd discovered her outside his window, a wraith in the night. He noticed that her hair was no longer pulled away from her forehead in the excruciatingly severe style she favored. A breeze from the Arabian Sea blew the strands across her face. Although the exact shade was still hidden by the shadows, he could tell that the length hung down her back and the ends caressed her waist.

Most contemporary women of fashion did not wear such a long style. Clearly, Crystal was not a woman of fashion. Her long hair was lovely. But the temptation to run his fingers through the glossy length annoyed him.

As his eyes adjusted from the light inside to the darkness of night, he noted further details about her. His pulse jumped when he realized she was dressed for bed. Her sleeping attire was high-necked and demure. Looking more closely, he saw that her nightgown was white, fashioned from satin and lace. Somehow that made it more erotic.

She wasn't wearing a robe—because she'd thought

she was alone? Life with his wife had taught him to question everything, and he wondered if Crystal truly hadn't known of his presence. Or if she had another agenda. But the manner in which she clung to the shadows hinted of a guileless quality that complemented the virginal image she portrayed in her innocent, high-necked nightgown. He swallowed hard, telling himself it was past time to go back inside. But he found that to do so required more energetic determination than he possessed just now.

Moving closer, he stopped just close enough to inhale the seductive scent of her skin.

"It's late," she said. "I'd better go in."

Her voice held a breathy, husky quality that he found pleasing and far too appealing. "Of course. You are still adjusting to the time difference. You must be tired."

"Oddly enough, I couldn't sleep."

"Then please stay," he said. "Keep me company."

What had made him ask that? It was unwise and foolhardy to voluntarily seek out a woman's company—any woman. What was it about this one that dissolved his common sense?

"Okay."

The single word spoken in her soft tone chafed his nerve endings. He shook his head. Enough of this nonsense. She was nanny to his children. He would discuss them with her.

"Hana and Nuri—are they asleep?"

She nodded. "Like little angels."

"I wish to thank you for taking their part tonight—with the king."

"You needn't thank me. They were behaving exactly like average five-year-olds and doing nothing wrong.

Your father has four children. He should understand that.''

"It has been many years since my brothers and sister and I were small. As my aunt said, he left our care to others.''

"Of course. Because he was busy running the country.'' She folded her arms over her bosom and leaned back against the wrought-iron railing.

"I am their father and protector. I should have intervened on their behalf.''

"It's difficult to know what behaviors are age appropriate when you're not trained in the care of children.''

"Miss Rawlins, is that an attempt to cut me some slack, as you Americans say?''

Her teeth flashed white when she smiled. "It's just the truth. Most fathers work and only see their children in the evening. It's the primary caregiver who knows them and can make a judgment about whether or not they're trying to pull a fast one.''

"Not my children,'' he said wryly.

"Of course not,'' she agreed. "It's a parent's job to think their children are perfect and work twenty-four/ seven to make it so. It will take me some time to get to know them. To interpret what they know and what they're capable of understanding. I don't believe it's right to hold them accountable for something if they can't comprehend what's expected of them.''

"They will be held to standards beyond those of the average child.''

"But they are still children,'' she protested.

"*Royal children.* Hana and Nuri will have many more pressures just because of who they are. More will be expected of them because of their high-born status.''

"Too much pressure will crush them if they're not prepared."

"It is your job to make certain that doesn't happen," he said.

"And I will do my best. But they will also need the influence and guidance of someone who's been where they are and knows how it feels."

"Someone like their father?"

"Yes," she agreed. "And their uncles. And aunt. Johara really has a way with children, an instinctive understanding and empathy."

"As do you." He slipped his hands into the pockets of his slacks. Her sensible approach and protectiveness toward his children pleased him.

"Thank you." She cleared her throat. "I was wondering why—"

"Yes?"

"They say curiosity killed the cat. But I can't help wondering what happened to the other nannies. Why five in a year?"

"It is wise to know the blunders of those who have gone before in order to avoid the same mistakes."

"I'll make new ones," she teased.

"Let us hope they are not beheading offenses."

"Let us hope you're kidding."

"I am." He laughed. "Let me see. The last nanny you already know about."

"I do. Rest assured I won't be showing up in anyone's bed unannounced."

"I'm relieved to hear it." Although a part of him wasn't so comforted. "One was homesick. Another the children disliked and the one after I disliked. And the last—" He thought, but the way Crystal's long hair blew across her face distracted him.

"Yes?"

"The last one ran off with the chauffeur," he finally said.

"So palace life is very much like a soap opera." She shook her head. "I can see why the king doesn't want another disruption."

"Speaking of disruptions, there is something else I wish to thank you for."

"Really? What?"

"Beauty is as beauty does," he said.

She nodded. "Vicki Rawlins's words of wisdom and useless advice."

"Vicki Rawlins?"

"My mother."

"Ah. Not so useless," he said. "If not for your mother's words, tonight blood would surely have been spilled. My brothers' to be exact."

She laughed and the sound was so pleasant it was impossible for him to keep from smiling with her.

"So, you think you could take both your brothers?"

"Undoubtedly. With one hand tied behind my back."

She laughed again. A lovely sound and one he seldom heard. At least not here on the balcony of his suite. He hadn't spent time here with a woman since long before his wife left. Crystal's present manner was also at odds with the paleness of her face when she'd agreed to have dinner with the royal family. Now he realized she'd found the prospect unnerving. But she'd managed to overlook her trepidation when she'd stood her ground to the king. And his brothers.

"I do hope dinner was not too great an ordeal for you," he commented. "When Rafiq issued the invitation, you looked as if you were going to your execution."

"It was fine. Easier than I'd expected," she said carefully. There was a sudden tenseness in her voice.

"What do you think of my family?"

"They remind me of my own. In fact that's one reason I jumped in to defend you. Memories of merciless piling on by my own brothers cranked up my sense of fair play. It surprised me because I thought—"

He leaned against the railing beside her, just far enough away to keep his arm from brushing hers. "What did you think?"

"It's probably inappropriate for me to say."

"Not if I wish you to. I promise not to hold your words against you."

"Like I believe that."

"You doubt me?"

"Of course."

He straightened to his full height and stared down at her. "I am a royal prince of El Zafir and sworn to honor the name of Hassan. If I do not speak the truth, may the fury of a thousand sand storms descend upon me."

"Wow. You certainly have a flair for the dramatic. Why shouldn't I trust you?"

"Indeed."

She sighed. "I was just going to say that I was nervous about meeting everyone in your family all at once because I thought wealth would make them different."

"Snobs?"

"Your word, not mine," she said cautiously. "But I was wrong. They're like any family who loves, respects and teases one another."

Pride and love for all of them expanded in his chest. "Position and wealth only change and enhance one's circumstances. It should not alter a person's basic nature, character and decency."

"I agree. Everyone made me feel comfortable and welcome. Even Johara seems to be a typical teenager. Eager for adventure and a bit outspoken. Although compared to teens where I come from, she held her tongue when ordered to."

"That is because in my country, not doing so could result in losing her tongue."

She gasped, then stared at him. "You're joking aren't you?"

"Yes."

She laughed. "I'm glad to hear it. But, seriously, Princess Johara is wonderful with your twins."

"The children adore my little sister."

"You're lucky she could fill in between nannies."

"Perhaps." He met her gaze. "But she's willful and rebellious." Too much like the children's mother for his peace of mind.

"She'll outgrow it."

"I hope you are right. But in the meantime, the children look up to her. She has a great deal of influence over them, and it concerns me that it could be unfavorable."

"I'm sure you're being overly anxious."

"Perhaps. In any case, it's fortunate that you have arrived to undertake their day to day care. Hana and Nuri took to you right away."

"I'm glad. Of course it's only a good thing if I'm a good role model," she teased.

"My instincts tell me you are a steady, sensible and extremely *honest* role model."

"I wouldn't stuff the family silver in my handbag, if that's what you mean."

"I wasn't implying that you would. In fact your background was thoroughly investigated."

"Naturally." Abruptly she straightened away from the railing.

"As is anyone who works in the palace. Aunt Farrah informed me there was nothing unexpected in the final report."

"Did she say anything else?"

"Only that you were perfect for me—that is, for the position."

"Good to know." She walked to the French doors, and light from inside highlighted the tension around her full lips. "Now if you'll excuse me, I think it's time for me to go inside. It's been a long day. And tomorrow I'm taking over the children's care full-time. Good night, Fariq."

Suddenly she was gone. He wondered if he'd said anything to offend her. But that was impossible. He'd spoken nothing but the truth as he always did. Truth and honesty were the greatest of life's prizes and beyond price.

This encounter with Crystal made him regret that he'd scheduled business meetings out of the country for the next several weeks. But he was pleased his children would be in the care of someone who was honest and steady.

For several seconds he stared at the spot where she'd stood just moments before. He'd enjoyed her companionship and suddenly felt very much alone. How could that be? Nothing of significance in his life had altered, yet he felt the solitude oppressive. Had it always been so? Or had he just never noticed until now?

Crystal cleared breakfast dishes from the table in Fariq's suite, then started loading them in the dishwasher. Pretending this was a luxurious, state-of-the-art condo instead of one of many rooms in a palace made her feel more comfortable. The kitchen wasn't so huge that walking it would give anyone a cardio workout, but the appliances had more bells and whistles than she'd ever seen. The granite countertops were basic brown with flecks of beige and black. In the center was an island with work space and a cooktop.

As she rinsed bowls and silverware, it occurred to her she'd passed the six-week mark in El Zafir and had loved every minute of it. The children seemed to thrive in the structured routine she'd set up for them.

Fariq had spent most of the time traveling, which puzzled her. The first of many business trips, interrupted by a night or two at home, had occurred the morning following their chance encounter on the balcony. His casual remark about her background investigation had sent her running like an evacuee from a forest fire. But when she'd calmed down, she'd realized if anything problematic had been discovered, she wouldn't have been hired.

She knew he traveled a lot, but somehow she hadn't expected him to leave right away. She'd thought he would wait until he was certain the children were comfortable with her. No question he was a busy, important man, but didn't charity begin at home? He had responsibilities to his offspring.

After that night when they'd talked in the dark, her female antennae were revved up and vibrating. Every night he phoned and after talking with the children, he spoke to her and asked for a report on their day. The conversations didn't diminish her fascination—in fact, they enhanced it. His deep, seductive voice was like a concentrated dose of sex appeal. When he talked, she could feel it from—

"Good morning."

There it was—the voice, butterscotch and brandy, that buzzed her nerve endings and raised tingles in places on her body where tingles could be the most dangerous. Turning from the sink, she met his black-eyed gaze. "Welcome back. When did you arrive?"

"Late last night." His gaze raked her from top to bottom, taking in her plain, long-sleeved white blouse and ankle-length navy skirt. "Where are the children?" he asked.

"I sent them to brush their teeth and wash their faces. Then they're off to the schoolroom."

He glanced at her, then the open door of the dishwasher. "What are you doing?"

"Dishes. The twins fixed their own oatmeal."

"You need only call the kitchen staff to see to your needs."

She rested her back against the sink as she dried her hands on a towel. "It's good for them to learn to do things for themselves. Gives them a sense of accomplishment."

"I see."

If he saw, then what was that funny look on his face about? "I wanted them to have a healthy breakfast and managed to come up with a combination of cinnamon, raisins, nuts and honey. They had fun making it."

"You could have the servants come in and clear the dishes."

"I know. But—" She nudged the glasses further up on her nose as she searched for a way to explain.

"What? Do you not recall that I promised not to hold your words against you?"

She remembered almost everything about that night. Like the masculine figure he'd cut with the sleeves of his dress shirt rolled up as he'd casually leaned against the railing. It had been dark. She'd worn only her night-gown. And his voice was so deeply soft and erotic he could have recited "Jabberwocky" and she would have been a puddle at his feet.

His extended absence had given her some peace of mind. But the children missed him terribly. And that bothered her.

"I'm trying to create an atmosphere for them that's—" she shrugged "—normal. Low-key. Give them a sense of proportion between their environment and the rest of the world. Does that make any sense?"

"Completely."

"I'm glad. I've developed a balanced curriculum for them, incorporating music and art with a teacher from the local university, along with reading, math and some foreign language lessons as you required."

Nodding, he leaned against the refrigerator and folded his arms over his chest. In his crisp white shirt the expanse appeared wide and firm. "It's important for them to be fluent in several languages."

"English being primary," she said, recalling the faxed memo she'd received from him. The man could use a little prioritizing in his own life—with his children a bit higher on the list. "I've developed some games to make the process fun. They hardly realize they're learn-ing. And they adore school. If I let them, I think they'd go seven days a week."

"And why do you not let them?"

At a loss how to answer, she simply stared at him. Then she saw the twinkle in his eyes. "It's called bal-ance. You could take lessons on that yourself."

"You're implying that I work too much?"

She shrugged. "If the shoe fits."

"Perhaps I've thrown myself too much into it since—"

"What?" she asked, noting the frown that chased the attractive gleam from his eyes.

"It's not important. But I wish to see the children now." There were squeals from the living room.

"And I believe I hear them coming." She grinned. "Am I good or what?"

"Papa!" Hana raced into the room carrying a stuffed panda. "Thank you for my present."

"Me, too," her brother said, right behind her with his own fuzzy animal.

The children waited until he held out his arms. Then they went to him and he folded them against his legs, bending to kiss the tops of their shiny dark heads. They were like little sponges soaking up any drop of affection he chose to give. Crystal wished he were around more. They clearly needed him. The achingly sweet scene launched a lump into her throat and she turned away to finish the dishes.

"Nanny made us oatmeal, Papa," Hana informed him.

"I like it," Nuri added.

"So she is a good cook?" There was a smile in his voice.

"Oh, yes," they said together.

"Maybe she will make some for me," he said, his voice low and deep.

Was there a double meaning in his words, she wondered. It was pretty certain she would never know. Folding the dish towel, she set it over the sink. "Hey, you two, it's time for school. You have music and art this morning with Miss Kelly. I'll walk you."

"Papa will you come, too?" Hana begged.

"Of course. I have missed you," he said. He smiled at his daughter, then looked up and met Crystal's gaze.

Had he missed her, too? What a ridiculous thought, but one she couldn't quite suppress after admitting to herself she'd noticed his absence more than a little.

He put on a double-breasted, pin-striped jacket before they left the suite. Since the children insisted on all of them holding hands, they walked four abreast down the hall to the area in the palace set up for class. Their teacher waited inside.

"I'm going to draw a picture for you, Nanny," Hana said when they stopped in front of the door.

"I would like that very much." Crystal bent and gave the child a hug and kiss. "What about you, young man? What are you going to do today?"

"I will learn a song to sing to you," he said solemnly.

"One of my very favorite things," she said, taking his face in her hands and kissing first one of his cheeks and then the other. His responding grin was so charming, so like his father's, her heart skipped then squeezed tight. She opened the door. "Now, it's time to go inside. Miss Kelly is waiting for you. I'll see you in a little while."

"Bye, Nanny," they both said, then walked into the suite waving their hands. "Bye, Papa."

The door closed and she was alone with Fariq. She felt compelled to fill the awkward silence. "You've just witnessed an example of our typical morning. The children have missed you very much."

"So much they draw and sing for you."

Uh-oh. How could she smooth ruffled royal feathers when she understood that the children were bonding with their primary care giver. "It's just you've been gone so much. It will take them a little time to warm up now that you're back."

"I do not wish to discuss this." He looked at his watch. "I must go."

Again? Irritation coursed through her. "Will you call the children tonight?"

"Why would I do that?"

"It's what you do every night."

"When I'm away on business," he clarified.

"So you're not leaving the country?" Why did her heart just skip like a stone across a lake?

"I am going to my office here in the palace."

She watched him walk in the direction of the business wing as her insides did a happy little dance because he wasn't going away. Instantly she put a stop to that reaction. It was a disaster in the planning stages.

She needed to focus on her job. It was time for her to go over the lessons and after-school activities for the children. She descended the staircase and went in the direction of the family wing, then stopped in front of the suite. Before she could go inside, a servant hailed her.

"What is it, Salima?" she asked the young, dark-eyed woman.

"Princess Farrah requests your presence right away, Miss Rawlins."

"Thank you. I'll go see her now."

The princess had a suite of rooms down the hall. Crystal had seen it on a number of occasions when she'd shared tea with the king's sister or brought the children for a visit with their great-aunt. She went in that direction thinking how quickly she'd become comfortable with her surroundings. At first she'd feared losing her way, never to be heard from again. It hadn't happened. Stopping in front of the door, she knocked and was instructed to enter.

The elegant foyer never failed to take her breath away, no matter how often she saw it. She'd been inside all the royal family's suites, since the children visited regularly with their relatives. It amazed her how different each was. Fariq's accommodated the children and was the only one with a kitchen. His bachelor brothers and father had rooms that were large and beautifully decorated, although without the needs of a family in mind.

But Princess Farrah's was the most elegant of all. The floor was marble with a circular cherrywood table standing in the center. On top, a crystal vase overflowed with fresh cut flowers that filled the area with a sweet fragrance. The living room contained priceless works of art.

"Your Highness?"

"In here, my dear."

The voice came from the living room, and Crystal went in that direction. Rounding the corner, she heard the woman mumble something that sounded like "absolutely no progress."

"Is something wrong, Your Highness?"

"Crystal." Princess Farrah, looking chic in a plum-colored designer suit, glanced up. "No, nothing's the matter. I'm just frustrated with a project I've been working on. Please sit down. Thank you for coming so quickly."

"You're welcome." She sat at a right angle to the woman on the semicircular white sofa that dominated the room. Across from it were the French doors that looked out on the Arabian Sea. "What is it I can do for you?"

"Actually, I wanted to talk about the children. I think—" A knock on the door interrupted her. "Come in."

Decidedly male footsteps sounded on the marble she'd just admired, then Fariq appeared. Crystal felt the pulse at the base of her throat flutter and folded her hands in her lap. Annoyingly, her palms were moist. Good grief, she'd just seen the man. But, she realized, her palms had been moist then, too. All her senses had returned to normal; now everything was going haywire again. He was like radiation to her Geiger counter.

He glanced from her to his aunt and bowed slightly. "Good morning."

"Nephew. Thank you for coming so quickly."

"You said it was regarding the children. I just left them. I hope there is nothing amiss."

"Do sit down." She smiled serenely. "Hana and Nuri are absolute angels. And Crystal is wonderful with them."

Crystal felt the sofa cushion dip from his weight. He sat so close beside her, she could lean slightly to her left and touch her lips to his cheek. The thought startled her. And it didn't help when Fariq slid a look in her direction as if he'd read her mind. Heat crept up her neck and flared in her cheeks. Life in the palace was so much simpler when he traveled.

Finally the princess' words of praise sank in, and she realized some kind of coherent reply was required, perhaps a thank-you for the compliment.

"Your Highness is very kind, but the children are just plain good kids. They're a joy to care for." Then a thought occurred to her. In Fariq's absence, especially right after her arrival, Crystal had taken instruction in her duties from the princess. Was there a major problem with the children that she needed to speak to both of them about?

"Is there something regarding Hana and Nuri that I'm unaware of? I'm completely open to suggestion, Your Highness. I don't mind. After all, you know them better than I. And they say it takes a village—"

She stopped babbling when Fariq reached over and touched a finger to her mouth, to silence her. The pulse in her throat, just calming down, jumped to life again and did a lively two-step.

He smiled at her. "Let us hear what my aunt has to say."

"Okay." She looked at the other woman. "Shoot. I mean, why did you send for me? Us," she amended sliding Fariq a glance.

The princess folded her hands in her lap. "Crystal, do you know how to ride a horse?"

The question was completely unexpected. "I've ridden a couple times, but I wouldn't say I possess any sort of proficiency. Is that a problem?"

The princess smiled with what looked like satisfaction. "Not at all. But I feel it is a skill you should master. For the children."

It was something she'd always wanted to do. How convenient. When duty and dreams collided, life was good. She didn't have a problem with that.

Beside her Fariq nodded thoughtfully. "I think I see what you mean, Aunt. And I agree. I will teach Crystal how to handle a horse. Personally."

Crystal stared at him. She had a problem with *that*.

Chapter Four

Beneath a clear blue sky, Fariq stood outside the stable and savored the fresh air. The scents of sand and sea mixed with the perfume of blooming jasmine touched a wellspring of pride deep inside him. He'd missed home. An exhilarating ride was just the thing after a great deal of time away on business. Exercise would be beneficial to body, mind and spirit.

After leaving his aunt, Fariq had ordered Crystal to change her clothes and meet him here. He'd left instructions at the stable for the horses to be saddled and waiting, then he'd had his assistant cancel and reschedule his morning appointments. Between Farrah and his sister, the children would be looked after when they returned from their lessons, giving him the afternoon to tutor the nanny in the fine art of riding a horse. He found the idea amusing and more pleasant than he would have imagined.

A familiar tightening inside warned of forming an attachment to a woman. Then a vision of her large

glasses and unflattering hairstyle made him laugh. There
was no threat of anything deeper. She quite successfully
met all the employment requirements. Suddenly, alarms
went off inside him again and he understood why. He'd
already given the woman more consequence than anyone he could recall in a very long time. Even when he'd
been away, he'd looked forward to their nightly phone
conversations regarding the children. He'd found her
throaty voice alluring and a pleasant distraction from
work.

And now that he was back home again, his interest
in her had increased. Especially as he watched her walking toward him down the stone path from the palace.
Against the salmon-colored stucco walls covered with
jasmine vines and hot-pink bougainvillea, she cut an
intriguing figure.

She wore a short-sleeved white blouse tucked into
appealingly snug jeans. The legs he'd unwillingly wondered about beneath her ankle-length hems were now
clearly defined in the worn denim. And the tempting
curves of her hips, thighs and calves exceeded his ex-
pectations.

Beside him, one of the horses snorted and restlessly
pawed the dirt with his hoof. Fariq reached over the
fence and rubbed his nose. "Patience, my friend. Soon
we will teach her everything she must know."

That thought stirred his blood, and he wondered at
the sensation. This was nothing more than his duty.
Making certain she was competent on horseback was in
the best interest of his children.

Her white tennis shoes stirred up dust as she stopped
beside him. With a knuckle, she nudged her sunglasses
up on her pert, freckle-splashed nose as she perused him.

"If I'd known we were going formal, I would have changed into my after-five jeans."

He glanced down at his full-sleeved, white silk shirt and tan riding breeches, then back at her. "I will see to it that you are provided with appropriate attire."

She gazed down. "What I'm wearing is inappropriate?"

Not as far as he was concerned. It was most becoming he decided, noting the way her small, firm breasts pushed against the cotton fabric of her blouse.

"As long as we stay within the confines of palace land it will do. If we stray further into the desert, it would be unwise not to have traditional garb. Today we will cover basics and will not go very far. As your skills improve and we venture from the grounds, security staff will accompany us."

"Is that necessary?" Her smooth brow furrowed with concern.

"Merely a precaution for me as a member of the royal family. I will let no harm come to you."

She didn't look completely reassured. "About that traditional attire. How will I know what's appropriate?"

He couldn't see the expression in her eyes because of her dark lenses, but a pulse fluttered at the base of her throat. She caught her top lip between her teeth, and he noted that her mouth was most lush and tempting. Odd. He hadn't noticed that before. Perhaps because her lack of cosmetics hadn't drawn his attention. But the nervous gesture definitely captured his notice. He wondered whether it was his warning or his presence that had made her so.

"Do not worry. As your employer, it is my responsibility to furnish whatever you require to perform your duties.'' He raised one eyebrow as he glanced at her feet. "Boots are essential.''

She glanced down at her feet and rocked back on the heels of her flimsy canvas shoes. "You're the expert. But a very busy one. Surely there is someone else who could teach me. Not that I don't appreciate your time, but is it really necessary for you to conduct this riding lesson?''

"I will do whatever possible to make certain my children are secure.''

"Whoa.'' She held up her hands. "Back up a step. I was curious when Princess Farrah mentioned it, but you moved so fast I didn't get a chance to ask. What does my competence on a horse have to do with the children?''

"Horsemanship is a genteel and royal recreation approved and encouraged by the king. At five years old, it is past the proper time for Hana and Nuri to acquire the skill. It is a part of their heritage and among the many things they will need to learn.'' He'd intended to initiate the lessons when the crisis arose with the last nanny. Between his business travel and the search for a replacement, riding had required an indefinite delay. "It is your job to oversee all their activities. Therefore you must be competent on horseback.''

"I won't be teaching them. Just along for the ride—so to speak.''

"Just so. Is it not reasonable that if you can't keep up with them, it is impossible for you to do a good job?''

"If it's part of the duties, why wasn't it on the list of requirements? Why didn't the job description call for a plain woman of some intelligence who can ride a horse?''

She shifted her weight and emerged from the shadow of the stable, allowing the afternoon sun to bring out the red highlights in her brown hair. The strands were pulled away from her face and secured at her crown with a large clip, creating a softer effect. He found the result quite charming.

"Earth to Fariq?"

"Hmm?" He straightened, struggling to concentrate on her words. Ah, the requirements. "It was not necessary to find a skilled horsewoman. Other considerations were more important, since your college degree proves you are trainable and capable of learning."

"But riding a horse is different from reciting facts from a book. It requires coordination. And a dash of athletic ability." She glanced up at the horses beside them, and a frown marred the smooth skin of her forehead. "And backbone."

"I'm unconcerned about that. Any woman who leaves everything familiar to travel and work in a land halfway around the world is not lacking in backbone."

"What about the nanny you lost to homesickness?"

"You are more mature than she. And I suspect you have an acute sense of adventure. Unless, of course, you lied."

She went suddenly still. "Excuse me?"

"To my aunt," he explained, wondering at her reaction. "Earlier when you said you wanted to learn to ride. Did you not tell the truth?"

"Oh. That." She released a long breath. "No. I would like very much to learn."

"Then your reluctance puzzles me."

"It's just that I'm uncomfortable about taking you away from more important things. Couldn't one of the grooms teach me?"

The lessons would require close and intimate personal contact. Another man put his hands on her? He rebelled at the thought. Because it was his duty to protect the employee responsible for his children. And for no other reason. But she seemed hesitant to spend time in his company. Could it be she found him displeasing?

Instantly he dismissed the idea. She'd given no indication of such a thing. In fact their encounters had been friendly and, he would swear, mutually engaging. He recalled her response when she'd told him of her personal agenda: travel, then love, marriage, children. Her vehemence had surprised him.

He studied her closely and saw the tension in her body, the still-fluttering pulse at the base of her throat. Could it be that his presence made her nervous? It was incomprehensible that she found him objectionable. Therefore it was reasonable to assume the opposite. She was attracted to him. Oddly, the thought pleased him.

"I will teach you to ride," he finally said. "I have rearranged my schedule in order to do so."

"But, Fariq—"

"I am the most competent horseman in the royal family although Rafiq would argue the point. And you are here to care for my children. Therefore it is my responsibility to instruct you—as a father and your employer." She opened her mouth to say something and he held up his hand. "I will hear no more on the subject."

"Okay. Then let's do it."

Finally. Capitulation. But he'd found the process invigorating. When was the last time he'd labored so strenuously to convince a woman to spend time in his company? More perplexing—when had it mattered to him that she did? Questions for which he had no answers. Nor did he wish to waste time finding them. Far more compelling was the prospect of touching her—in the context of teaching her. And he couldn't help being grateful to his aunt for suggesting this opportunity.

"First you must become acquainted with your mount. This is my horse, Midnight," he said, sliding his hand over the black stallion's neck, then patting him. Fariq pointed to the light-colored yellow-brown one beside her. "That is Topaz. She was chosen carefully for your personal use. She is gentle-natured and will serve you well. A true jewel."

Like Crystal? Precious, yet hard and strong. Able to withstand the harsh conditions of the desert? Time would tell.

Without hesitation she raised her hand and rubbed the horse's nose, then imitated his movements, stroking and petting. The animal nuzzled her shoulder affectionately.

She laughed. "I think maybe we just bonded. You're a good girl," she crooned, then glanced inside the shaded interior. "I've toured the facilities. And I bet she's a happy girl, considering these elegant surroundings. I'm no expert, but aren't the stalls made of mahogany?"

"Yes. It is quite durable."

Almost reverently Crystal brushed her palm over her horse's saddle blanket and the royal crest fashioned from red, green and gold threads. "Very nice."

"The stables are climate controlled for comfort, and the watering troughs are automatic and fashioned from stainless steel."

"State-of-the-art stable," she commented. "Those horses only need a microwave and a high-definition big-screen TV. There are people—maybe even some in this country—who would give anything to live a horse's life here in the royal stable. Although that whole mono-dietetic oats thing could be a little monotonous.''

Fariq was mesmerized by her teasing smile and the way it transformed her face, making it almost beautiful. He forced himself to concentrate on her words instead. The tone she'd used was pleasant but laced with barbs. Something nettled her.

''The animals here are priceless purebreds. It's no more than common sense to protect the investment and care for them in the best environment.''

''What about the average citizen in this country? Are they taken care of?''

Ah. A liberal—or as she'd called herself—a Republicrat. One who had much to learn—and not only about riding a horse. ''We have many programs to help the people.''

''I'm glad to hear it.'' Pointedly she traced the intricate carving on the horse's silver bridle and looked at him. ''When do I get to sit on her?''

Apparently she chose not to pursue that line of conversation.

''Now, if you're ready.'' He checked the saddle on her horse, making sure it was secure. Then he turned his back to see to his own animal. ''Remember to always mount from the left. Put your left foot in the stirrup and swing your right leg over her rump.''

''Okay.''

He heard the creak of leather and glanced over his shoulder to find her sitting atop Topaz, smiling broadly down at him. ''I missed your technique, but I see that it was successful,'' he said.

''I grew up watching those B-Westerns we talked about. Some of it must have sunk in.''

"Apparently." He experienced a vague feeling of disappointment that she hadn't needed his assistance.

After eyeing the length of her stirrups to find they needed no adjustment, he swung up into his own saddle trying to shake off another deflated sensation. "Take both reins loosely in your left hand," he said. Glancing at her he saw she'd already done so.

"Then I just move my hand in the direction I want her to go, right? And pull back gently if I want her to stop. Grip with my knees and thighs."

"Yes." When he nudged his mount forward, Topaz fell into step.

"How about them apples? I guess all those hours of watching TV weren't wasted."

He frowned.

She looked at him and grinned. "Does that look frighten women and small children, Fariq?"

"I have no look. I do not know what you mean."

She rode beside him, but too far away to touch. "If you say so."

"Do you doubt me?"

"That's a loaded question. If I say yes, you might feel compelled to lie and risk the fury of a thousand sandstorms. I'm not sure I want to be collateral damage." She shook her head. "Therefore, I have no doubt."

"I never lie."

"Never?" she asked. "Surely you don't believe that sometimes it can be the lesser of two evils? A kinder thing to do? If your aunt asked you whether or not her latest designer suit made her derriere look big, what would you say?"

"The truth. Anything less would be dishonest, a character flaw I abhor."

"I agree that certain things demand absolute veracity but sometimes small details are unimportant to the big picture. Why are you so rigid—"

"The reasons are unimportant. What is imperative for you to know is that I despise it in others and do not permit it in myself."

"I see," she said.

No. There was no way an innocent like Crystal could know the manner in which his wife had taught him how priceless the truth. The woman was out of his life, but the scars would always remain. The only good thing she'd given him was his children. They were everything to him. From them and all the children of El Zafir he gleaned the passion to make his country successful, valued in the new world order. To do that, he needed to solidify the El Zafirian economic base.

Man did not support himself through oil alone. Fariq was determined to diversify their financial interests. And it required meetings in other countries. Just that morning, Crystal had spoken critically about his frequent absences and the fact that Hana and Nuri had no mother. But if she'd known Fatima, she would understand that they were better off. She would also know why Johara's wild streak and influence on his children was a source of concern.

Glancing beside him, he noticed Crystal had grown quiet and tense. Her full mouth, so tempting moments before, was pulled into a straight line. Her body was rigid and she looked as if she might shatter. Topaz shifted restlessly.

"Relax," he said. "You're doing quite well."

"Thanks," she answered, without meeting his gaze.

It was fortunate she required little instruction. His thoughts had taken a turn, distracting him from their conversation. What had they been discussing? Ah, yes. His sincerity. She'd said she had no doubts.

But he had some. Most of them about his sanity. Because he found he wanted to stroke away her unease and return the smile to her face. He wanted to touch her. He hadn't realized how much he'd anticipated doing so until her athletic aptitude had denied him at every turn. She took to the horse like a camel to the desert. He wished for Rafiq's glib tongue and easy way with women. The more he wrestled with those thoughts, the more he feared his frown *might* frighten women and children. So they rode in silence.

What was that American saying? "I touch the world, I teach." Not in his experience this day. Something he found damnably frustrating. The truth unsettled him. But the fact remained that he must fight his temptation to discover the shape and texture of the curves she'd finally revealed to him.

After just an hour on horseback, Crystal's backside felt black and blue, not to mention the tender area along the insides of her thighs. When she was on terra firma again, she had a feeling her legs would hold her up about as well as a couple of wet noodles. She also noticed tightness in her arms, hands and shoulder muscles. But that could have something to do with tensing up.

Following Fariq's declaration that he never lied, they had ridden in silence for a while. Every woman knew men compromised the truth. Why did she have to work for the only one on the planet who didn't speak with a forked tongue? Her guilt had weighed heavily, and she'd debated whether or not to tell him her secret. Payments to her mother had satisfied creditors and prevented the sale of her home. But there were still a mountain of medical bills to pay.

Then she thought of the children. Five nannies in a year. Until her arrival, they'd been shuffled back and forth between servants and family members—whoever had time for them. Now they seemed happy and content. Was it fair to rock their boat right now?

Finally she'd decided to give it more time. When their father could see she was good for them, she would come clean and hope he'd understand. He might perceive her behavior less than honorable. But wasn't the welfare of his children the right reason? In the meantime, she would sacrifice her body for her job. But what a way to go.

Earlier, she'd begged Fariq to let her go faster and he'd agreed. She couldn't remember the last time she'd had so much fun. And he'd looked like he was enjoying himself, too. But his eyes reminded her of twin hot coals, and tension almost emanated from him.

"You did quite well for your first lesson." He slid her a look, and something glittered in his eyes. "Your hair is coming down."

He'd just noticed? The bouncing had caused her hair to slip from the clip a long time ago. With the very urgent need to hang on to the reins, there hadn't been a whole lot she could do about it.

"I should have secured it better."

But the look in his eyes said he disagreed. "There is color in your face again. Your cheeks are quite pink. You enjoyed the ride?"

"Very much," she enthused.

He halted Midnight right outside the stable. With cat-like grace, he swung his muscular leg over the horse's rump as he dismounted. After looping the reins over the fence, he took hers and did the same.

Turning back, he looked surprised to see her still sitting in the saddle. After several moments, a slow half smile turned up the corners of his mouth. "It is one thing to watch a Western, it is quite another to star in one, is it not?"

"If you're asking whether or not my backside is unhappy, the answer would be a resounding yes." When his smile grew wider, she scowled at him. "And you needn't look so pleased about it."

He rested his hands on lean hips. "I am not pleased. That would be ungentlemanly, not to mention ungracious. Unfortunately, when one learns to ride, it takes a toll on one's muscles—in certain vulnerable areas. Until you become used to the saddle, it is a distressing side effect." Coming around to her left side, he held out his arms. "I will help you down."

"Thanks, but I can do it."

She hung on to the saddle horn and lifted her right leg to dismount, then sort of let her quivering muscles take advantage of gravity until both her feet were on the ground. There, that part wasn't so hard. After reluctantly releasing her grip on the saddle, she turned unsteadily and started to take a step. That part was hard. When she stumbled, Fariq reached out and easily caught her.

"Perhaps I kept you out too long for your first lesson."

"I was having a wonderful time. Besides, I think it wouldn't have mattered how long we rode. My vulnerable areas would still be cursing you."

Other vulnerable areas were far too happy to be nestled against his broad chest. The pressure of his strong arms holding her to him and his hard muscular thighs pressed to hers started a different sort of trembling in her that had nothing to do with her riding lesson. Her heart fluttered, then kicked in and pumped as if she'd just passed mile thirteen in a marathon.

He gave her a rueful smile. "Still, I should have been more sensitive to your inexperience. I promise to make it up to you."

How? When the look in his eyes grew hotter, she feared she'd asked the question out loud. But she hadn't. And he continued to stare at her as if she were a particularly desirable and delectable piece of chocolate. Like fire, the dark, dangerous expression on his face stole the oxygen from her lungs. It robbed her of the ability to think, let alone move.

In the next instant, he lowered his head to capture her mouth. A jolt arced through her, as if she'd touched an exposed electrical wire and fried all her mental circuits. That was the only explanation for the soft, needy moan trapped in her throat.

With a harsh, almost growling sound, he slid his tongue into the moist interior of her mouth with a single sure thrust. Stunning sensation skipped along her nerve endings to her breasts then her fingertips and all the way to her toes, leaving in its wake a fluttery, feverish feeling. His breathing grew ragged as he snuggled her more securely into his embrace. Pressed together from knee to shoulder, her breasts flattened against the solid wall of his chest. She felt the powerful muscles in his thighs. And she was both shocked and thrilled at the evidence of his desire.

When he moved his hand up to cup her cheek and tangle his fingers in her hair, she gloried in the touch. His thumb caressed her jaw, and she swore sparks flew from the friction. Any second she expected to go up in flames, and for the life of her, she couldn't seem to care. And all the while, his lips held hers prisoner.

His probing fingertips connected with the rim of her sunglasses. He raised his head, severing the bond of their questing mouths. Instantly she missed the warmth and connection.

He frowned down at her as his chest rose and fell, his breathing uneven. "You are full of surprises. As passionate and bright and mysterious as the desert."

Her heart was racing and her pulse pounded in her ears. She didn't know what to say. "Fariq, I—"

He let out a long breath as he touched the rim of her sunglasses. "My little jewel of the desert— Let me see your eyes."

He was going to take off her glasses? Suddenly adrenaline rushed through her, putting her mental circuits back on line. She backed away from him, out of the circle of his arms. Her skin was clear of everything but sunscreen. Not a speck of makeup. But her hair was hanging around her face and she didn't have on her long, shapeless clothes. Sunglasses were the only part of her disguise in place, her last defense. And defense was definitely what she needed.

An unassuming appearance was supposed to keep the lid on palace shenanigans. The king disapproved of hanky-panky with the hired help. So what the heck was that kiss all about? And who would get the blame for it? No one at the palace had accused her of being too attractive. And now this.

"I...I have to go."

"Not yet. Let me—"

She shook her head. "I have to relieve Johara. The twins will wonder where I am."

"They know you are with me." He frowned as he shuffled his boots in the dirt.

"But this happened so fast." And she didn't just mean the riding lesson. "I...I mean I didn't have a chance to prepare them ahead of time for my absence," she said, starting to turn away.

"Wait." He reached out a hand. When he saw it was trembling, he closed his fingers into a fist. His eyes were dark and unreadable when he said, "I have made you uncomfortable."

"Yes— No— I—"

"It will not happen again."

Did that mean he was going to fire her?

He ran a hand through her hair. "But I do not regret discovering that there are many more facets to you than I guessed. I look forward to learning more of them."

She let out a long breath. The good news was she wasn't going to lose her job. The bad news—he wanted to find out more about her. And she knew he would.

Because he never lied. The thought sent a shiver rushing through her at the same time she realized she couldn't let it happen. "I've been thinking. Since my lesson today went so well, maybe I could just practice by myself from now on?"

He shook his head. "There is more instruction I must give you."

The way her heart hammered now, she was afraid to think about what kind of education he had in mind. "But I still feel I'm taking you away from your other, more pressing matters."

What else could be more pressing than the tender way he'd held her? Obviously his kiss had produced a brain meltdown since there was no other explanation for her thinking in double entendres.

"On the contrary. Time is of the essence. In two weeks you must be proficient enough to accompany the children and I into the desert. There is something of importance I must attend to and I wish Hana and Nuri to go along. Therefore I require your presence."

"I see."

Crystal's eyes widened, and she was grateful he couldn't see. When he dropped his hand, she resisted the urge to rub the warm place where his strong fingers had held her. Surely the heat had branded her forever. Alarmed at her reaction and inability to control it, she whirled away from him. With a great deal of self-restraint, she kept herself from running back to her room. With enough distance his spell over her disappeared, and she realized he hadn't said he was sorry. She couldn't help being glad about that even though he probably never apologized for anything.

And she didn't want him to now. From the time boys had discovered her, she'd been judged by outward appearances. He'd kissed her in spite of the way she looked. And it had felt awfully wonderful. She couldn't be sorry.

But she was in trouble. The only questions—how big and was it irreparable?

Chapter Five

It had been two weeks since Fariq had kissed the daylights out of her.

As Crystal rode her horse behind his into the desert, she realized that her standard of marking time had been forever altered to before the kiss and after. Before was your basic ignorance-is-bliss scenario, because no other man had ever kissed her like that. And after? That was hell, because now she knew how wonderful it felt.

Ever since, she'd wondered why she hadn't demanded an explanation for his actions on the spot. It always came back to the fact that she'd been too anxious to keep him from removing her glasses. But that didn't explain why he'd kissed her when she'd done everything possible to disappear off his radar.

She'd expected him to blame her for it, but he'd never said a word. Never even brought up the subject. Never said he was sorry. Never kissed her again.

Unfortunately, there was a reason for that and it was pretty humiliating. He'd been unimpressed with her.

And his grand declaration about getting to know her better was just so much hot air. Because if he'd wanted to, there had been ample opportunity. They'd spent every afternoon riding together. Sometimes the children came along for their own instruction. But frequently they were alone so that he could make sure she was ready for the big outing. Eventually he'd told her they were going to the oasis for some mysterious, traditional thing he did.

Now here she was, following him as ordered. His security staff surrounded them—some on horseback, others in all terrain vehicles—all of them positioned at a discreet distance. Excitement hummed through her at the adventure of it all, the chance to rough it in the wilds of El Zafir. She couldn't wait to e-mail her mother with the spine-tingling details.

Tingle number one: watching Fariq riding with his children. He was so tender with them. Each child had started out on their own mount until fatigue set in, then he'd put them in one of the security vehicles. She was glad the children would be reunited with them when they arrived. Because Fariq might not want another mouth-to-mouth go-round, but she was sure tempted. Twin chaperones would nip that little problem in the bud.

Tingle number two: the mystery of it all. The destination was never in question. But the purpose was shrouded in secrecy. She'd been unable to coax even a hint of their mission from Princess Farrah. The woman had merely looked perplexingly pleased when Crystal had mentioned the upcoming trip.

She was bursting with curiosity as she nudged her horse to go a little faster and came up alongside Fariq. "Are we there yet?"

He glanced at her, and the sudden power and appeal of his grin tilted her world. She gripped the saddle horn to keep from falling off. Obviously, he'd recognized her imitation of his children, who had no frame of reference for arrival time.

"Soon."

It had been his standard response to the twins since ten minutes after leaving the stables. As nearly as she could tell, they'd been traveling for close to two hours.

She looked at the panorama of the desert, marveling at the stark beauty. "And we can't even play the license plate game."

"What game is this?"

"On a long car trip, my parents used to keep the five of us entertained by looking for all the letters of the alphabet on the license plates of passing cars."

He followed her gaze. Since the vehicles were too far away to see clearly, there was nothing much there but sand. "No, that is not possible here."

She shifted in the saddle and marveled that she was getting used to the exercise and wasn't sore. Practice makes perfect, she thought. And her traditional clothes were wonderfully comfortable.

"I like my appropriate attire," she said. "You were right."

"Of course." One corner of his wonderful mouth lifted. "About what?"

"The boots are definitely a help. My feet don't slip in the stirrups now."

"The traditional El Zafirian garb suits you."

A glow started inside her at his words. When she'd first tried the clothes on, she thought she'd never get used to all the layers. She wore a white robe that fell to her feet with a hood to cover her hair. A detachable veil was hooked in place to hide her face. Beneath this outer garment, she had on loose-fitting trousers and a matching long-sleeved, high-necked shirt made from a soft, lightweight and very luxurious weave of cotton. It had looked stifling, but proved incredibly cool.

She smiled. "I don't think the fashion police would share your opinion that it suits me, but that's their problem. This is probably the most comfortable outfit I've ever worn. Your country is light-years ahead in the sunscreen department. There's no way the UV rays are getting through all these layers of material."

"And the boots are satisfactory, as well?"

She nearly sighed in ecstasy. The leather was soft and supple, almost caressing her feet. And as she'd already said, eminently practical. "Oh, yeah. Definitely satisfactory."

"I am glad they please you." He guided his mount to the vehicle in which his children were riding.

"Are we there yet, Papa?" Hana asked again through the open window.

"Yes, Papa," Nuri chimed in. "My tushy hurts."

Fariq looked at her as one eyebrow rose. "Tushy?"

"It's an American expression for vulnerable parts."

"I have heard it." He looked at his son. "It will not be long."

"There," Crystal said, pointing as they crested the sand dune alongside the all-terrain vehicle. "It looks like an oasis and tent to me."

"Ya-ay!" both children called out.

With her own excitement barely contained, Crystal scanned the scene as they lumbered over the dune. Palm trees dotted the area, along with lush vegetation and a small lake. In the center was a large, sturdy-looking tent. Just beyond it was a satellite dish she figured was for communication purposes and not HBO.

"What's that?" she asked pointing to a large shed next to the dish.

"A generator for climate control."

"So this is roughing it, El Zafirian style," she said dryly. When would she remember to think outside the box where the royal family was concerned?

She was surprised to see a good number of people milling around the open area in front of the compound.

She looked at Fariq. "Apparently word of your visit leaked out."

"Not a leak," he said. And mysteriously neglected to add more by way of explanation.

Before she could ask, they stopped and were surrounded by four members of his security team. She was helped to dismount and, along with Fariq and the children, escorted inside the tent. He suggested she look around and took the children off with him.

After several moments her eyes adjusted to the interior after the brightness outside. Then all she could think was wow! The tent was bigger than she'd first thought; huge, in fact, and partitioned into rooms. Silk hangings decorated the walls, costly Persian rugs were arranged on the floor and colorful, cushy pillows covered low white sofas scattered throughout. As she strolled through she saw that there were bedrooms and bathing facilities.

When she worked her way back to where she'd started exploring, she saw a wooden table and chairs that rivaled the one in the palace dining room. Running her finger over the polished teak, she noticed the legs were carved with what looked like scenes. The pieces were rubbed to a high gloss and quite lovely. She continued strolling until she arrived at the largest area, which would have been a ballroom anywhere else. It was without furniture except for a wooden chair set up at one end with a line of people waiting in front of it. She was reminded of the mall Santa at Christmas.

Fariq stopped beside her. "It is time to begin."

"Begin what?" she asked, as the children each grabbed on to one of her hands.

"You will see." He pointed to a pile of cushions next to the chair. "Bring the children and sit there."

"Okay."

Feeling as wide-eyed as the twins, Crystal did as instructed and settled them on the soft, comfortable seat. Trustingly, they nestled one on each side of her, and out of the blue, a lump jumped into her throat. It surprised her how quickly she'd come to care for these two, and all her protective instincts cranked into high gear. Especially when she noticed the curiosity they'd generated in the line of people waiting. The staring made her feel uncomfortable.

A man stood behind her. "I am Khalid, aide to Prince Fariq. He has requested me to interpret for you."

She started to ask what was happening, but he shushed her with a finger to his lips. A man stepped before Fariq and bowed at the waist. In what she assumed was native El Zafirian, he spoke long and earnestly. Fariq listened attentively then answered in the unfamiliar language. A huge grin spread over the man's face and he bowed again before backing away.

"What happened?" she asked Khalid.

"The man's wife is with child. She has miscarried twice before and there are again difficulties. He must transport her to the capital city for continuing medical care. When it's time for the birth, he wants the baby born in the new hospital Prince Kamal is building."

"Will it be ready in time?" she asked, concerned.

He nodded. "It will open shortly. This man hasn't a reliable vehicle to make so important a journey."

"Then what will he do?" Crystal asked.

"The prince just gave him one," Khalid said seriously.

Her eyes widened. "Just like that? Fariq gave away a car?"

"Yes."

"This isn't even *The Price is Right*—"

He shushed her again when another person stepped before Fariq. Crystal watched the earnest appeal of a man who looked to be in his mid-thirties. Because she didn't understand the words, she studied Fariq. Her heart beat a little faster when she realized how handsome he looked in his traditional clothing. The cotton trousers and shirt with sash at the waist definitely suited him. He looked like a three-dimensional definition of *romantic rogue*.

Watching the emotions on his face, she noticed the gleam in his dark eyes. She swore he was holding back a grin. But he continued to listen intently. Finally he spoke and the serious expression on the stranger's face disappeared, replaced by a broad smile as he bowed and backed away. Obviously, his wish had been granted. She could hardly wait for the translation.

"Khalid, what—"

"He requested a loan. It is his intention to start a furniture business."

"And, just like that, the prince feels the man is a good risk?"

"His concern is not the success or failure of the venture. Prince Fariq made a gift of more money than requested. His only stipulation was to employ as many as possible. His objective is to give his people a means of earning a living for their families.''

''Wow.''

She started to say to the children that their father was the El Zafirian equivalent of Santa Claus and the good fairy all rolled into one. But when she glanced down, she saw that they were asleep, each with a cheek resting on one of her legs. Obviously the ride had wiped them out. Fatigue, not fascination, had rendered them speechless. So she left them to rest as the process went on and on.

Fariq granted requests ranging from money for burdensome medical bills to funds for college to more capital for business ventures. Khalid explained it was more than mere generosity. The prince wanted to diversify the country's economy and it was economically sound to put people to work. The whole procedure was fascinating to her. And from the expression on his face, Fariq loved every minute of this job.

For the second time that day, emotion bubbled inside her. She'd understood what she felt for the children. This feeling for their father was far more complicated. *Inappropriate* and *untimely* were two adjectives that instantly came to mind. And that was one spine-tingling and potentially worrisome detail she wouldn't be sharing with her mother. Because Crystal had no intention of allowing her obviously one-sided, dead-end attraction to become a problem.

The following morning outside the tent, Fariq kissed Hana and Nuri goodbye then handed them into the SUV with the driver/bodyguard who would deliver them safely to the palace.

"Be good for Aunt Farrah," he said to Nuri.

"Yes, Papa," the boy answered. "But when is Nanny coming home? I have something I need to show her."

"It is her day off. You must wait."

"Why does she need a day off?" he asked.

Fariq grinned at his son. "Because you two keep her very busy and she must take some time to rest."

"We just play with her. She is more fun that Aunt Farrah."

"Yes," his sister agreed. "Almost as fun as Aunt Johara. But I like Nanny best."

Fariq liked her, too. More than he wanted to admit. Since he'd kissed her, he'd been able to think of little else. The daily riding sessions had been torture as he'd struggled with his yearning to do so again. That first day, if he hadn't been so frustrated by his inability to touch her, he would have been able to resist the temptation to know whether or not her lips were as soft and responsive as they looked. He regretted that he'd sent her running like a scared rabbit, but it was difficult to be contrite when she'd rewarded him with such a passionate response.

Yesterday he'd surreptitiously watched her as he'd listened to his people's petitions. His intention had been to impress her, but he had yet to understand why it was important to do so. Now he was most curious to find out if he'd succeeded.

He sighed as he gazed at his children. "I'm glad you like Nanny. And do you wish her to be happy with us?"

"Yes," both children agreed.

"As do I. So we must see that she has the opportunity to rest."

"Who's resting?"

He turned and saw Crystal emerge from the tent. She wore her robes, and the veil hid face. But her eyes, even behind her glasses, were alight with humor. Dancing, he thought as his stomach tightened in warning.

"You are," he said. "At least it was my intention that you should."

"Nanny, we are going to Aunt Farrah so you can be happy," Nuri said.

Hana nodded. "Papa says you need to rest."

He shook his head at his children. They sometimes seemed two halves of a whole. To get across a complete idea, both of them had to put their thoughts together.

Crystal walked to the vehicle. "I'm not tired. If you need me I'll go with you."

The children shook their heads, and like a good little martyr Nuri said, "We'll find someone else to play with."

"I'm sure your Aunt Johara will entertain you," she suggested.

They nodded. "Goodbye, Nanny."

Crystal hugged them both. "Be good."

Fariq frowned as the door was closed and his driver whisked them away. The mention of his sister's name made him uneasy. Johara's mother had been much like his wife—wild and selfish. He felt more serene when his daughter was in Crystal's care. But by contract she was entitled to one full day and an afternoon off a week. Aunt Farrah had scolded him because Crystal never took the whole time. She went into the capital city once a week for an errand, but immediately returned to the palace. She was constantly with the children, but today he would change that.

"So," she said, looking up at him. "I guess we'll ride the horses back to the palace?"

"Yes." He folded his arms over his chest. "But first, would you care for a guided tour?" He extended his arm in a gesture that indicated the desert.

"Very much," she said.

Fariq saw the smile in her eyes. He felt more satisfaction in seeing her pleased than he did from all the supplications he'd granted the previous day. Which was most perplexing.

"Very well. The horses are waiting for us." He saw doubts in her gaze as she glanced back at the tent.

"What happens to it? Is it all right to leave it?"

He nodded. "It is permanent, with a full-time staff. My father keeps it as a symbol of our nomadic ancestry. My brothers and I like to come here to clear our heads."

"A modest little getaway?"

"Just so," he said grinning.

He smiled often in her presence, he realized. Perhaps that was the reason he wished to spend time with her. It had nothing to do with her avid response to his kiss. Although the image of her from two weeks before was still vivid in his memory. Her beautiful hair a silken curtain of shimmering mahogany highlights in tousled disarray around her face. She looked as if she'd just come from a man's bed. He'd been unable to resist the temptation she'd presented. Even now, with her hair covered and only the twinkling of her eyes visible to him, he grew aroused at the memory. How curious.

"Let us go."

They mounted their horses and he led the way, circling the oasis. He told her about the natural underground spring that supported the lush plants, trees and flowers. For thousands of years his people had relied on its bounty for life. It was a mark of their resilience and determination to survive. He explained all of this as pride in his country and heritage swelled in his chest.

"Of course once oil was discovered, economic considerations changed."

"I guess so," she said dryly. "Speaking of which, what was that all about yesterday?"

"I spoke of it on the day you had your first riding lesson. It is one of the programs that benefit my people."

"You should have elaborated. I feel like an idiot for insinuating the horses were better cared for than the people."

"I thought it would have more impact if you saw for yourself."

"Show don't tell. Definitely an impact," she agreed. "I need to apologize for thinking what I thought."

"There is no need. This desert tradition was begun by my grandfather and passed down to my father and now me. One day I will relinquish the privilege to Nuri."

"But he's only five. Isn't he too young?"

"Traditionally it is the age when royal children begin learning about their culture, customs and all that will be expected of them."

"So that's why you wanted the twins here. And me with them."

He nodded. But it didn't explain why he now wanted her here without the children. He should have learned. The dangers of the desert were nothing compared to the jeopardy posed by a woman. But this woman surely posed no threat. After careful consideration, his aunt had said she was perfect.

But if that was so, why had he been so exhilarated by her eager acceptance of his offer to ride this day? His wife would never have agreed to the invitation. It was a nasty pastime in her opinion, too dirty and windy. Her hair and cosmetics would have been compromised.

Surely his suggestion of a ride was nothing more than courtesy to Crystal who was a guest in his country as well as his employee. What more could it be, he thought, gazing at the barren, unforgiving sands beyond the oasis? The desert was like a woman. When its danger struck, one learned not to make the same mistake. He would play gracious host, quickly show her the sights as promised, then lead the way back to the palace where he would no longer be alone with her.

Crystal looked at him. "Tell me about this tradition where you grant wishes."

Good. A neutral topic. "My grandfather believed the people should share in the wealth. Twice a year he met with them to hear and grant their petitions."

"I'm surprised there weren't more people. You could be stuck there for days hearing everyone's requests."

He smiled. "The process did get out of hand and forced us to revise it. All the requests must now be submitted in writing for screening. Only those with merit are invited to the oasis."

"So they know ahead of time that the wish will be granted?"

"No."

"But everyone who shows up does get what they asked for?"

"Yes."

"You're a fraud."

"How so?"

She studied him, then looked straight ahead as her body swayed with the horse's gait. "You're aloof, acting as if you don't care. Yet you play fairy godfather."

He wasn't especially comfortable with the fairy part, but he understood the reference. "It is my job."

"And you love it."

He took great pains to conceal his emotions and hadn't been aware they were so readily discernible. It was disconcerting that this woman had seen what he was feeling.

"It is my job," he said again.

"Why do you hide the fact that you're a softie?"

Before he could respond, a strong gust of wind swirled the sand up and around them. The sudden whirling grit along with the flapping material in her robe startled the horses into restlessness. The animals were accustomed to riding in the desert. Fariq had learned never to ignore their instincts and behavior, which warned of something he could not yet see. When her horse continued to dance uneasily, he reached over to grab the bridle and soothe the beast even as the wind picked up.

He met her gaze. "We must go back to the oasis at once. Sandstorms come up unexpectedly in the desert."

"Shouldn't we go back to the palace? Wouldn't we be safer there?"

"Yes. But we would never make it in time. We must hurry and take shelter. Just in case," he said.

"How long before we can start back to the palace?"

"Maybe a few hours."

She shrugged. "That's not so bad."

"Or longer," he added.

"We could be here overnight?"

"Maybe more than one. But do not be concerned. You will be safe. I promise no harm will come to you."

The fearful look in her eyes was tinged with innocence and had compelled him to issue the vow. His promise was instantly followed by a powerful urge to take her in his arms. Which he would not do. So he swore on the honor of his ancestors to protect her from the elements.

Because, of course, she was safe from him.

Chapter Six

Crystal threw back the bedcovers wondering which god she'd ticked off and how she could make amends.

Shuddering, she listened to the wind howling outside and flinched as grit and sand pelted and pushed against the tent. Before the storm, the expensively furnished interior could make her forget that she wasn't in the palace with sturdy walls around her. Not anymore. Now Mother Nature was waving her atmospheric wand with a forceful reminder that the only thing standing between her and the elements was flimsy material.

Crystal turned on the bedside lamp, then grabbed her robe. The storm had increased in intensity after they'd returned to the oasis and taken shelter. Fariq had notified his family that they were staying put. Then he'd spent the rest of the day working, but she'd been at loose ends since the children had returned to the palace. Fortunately this modest royal getaway spot boasted a well-stocked library.

The staff had insisted on preparing dinner, then Fariq

had finally convinced them to go home to their families in case the storm grew more intense. The two of them had eaten at the beautifully carved table she'd admired yesterday. Had it only been a day? It seemed much longer. Afterward, Fariq had once again buried himself in work. She hadn't realized she'd looked forward to spending time with him until it hadn't happened.

And why should it? She was the hired help. If a fluke of nature hadn't landed them in this predicament, she would be back at the palace checking on the children, not out in the desert alone with their father. To take the edge off her disappointment and loneliness, she'd re-tired with a book to the same bedroom she'd slept in the night before. Between the wind's mournful wail and the way it made the tent walls snap, the storm kept her awake better than a shot of caffeine. Every time she started to drift off, a particularly vicious gust would attack. If you can't beat 'em, get up and read, she thought.

"I saw your light."

Startled, Crystal looked up to find Fariq in the door-way. "I didn't know you were still awake."

Fortunately she'd been preparing to read and had on her glasses. But her hair was down. She tugged the la-pels of her robe more tightly across her breasts. As if that would really do anything constructive to restore her disguise.

He was still dressed in loose cotton pants and shirt. The sash was gone, but his dark wavy hair and the shadow of his unshaven jaw still made him look like a rogue.

"Are you all right?"

"I couldn't sleep," she admitted. "I keep wondering

if any minute I'll wind up airborne, like Dorothy in *The Wizard of Oz*."

A slow half smile curved his mouth. "If memory serves, that was a tornado. This is a sandstorm. Very different and quite common in this part of the world."

"It's all your fault, you know."

"Excuse me?" he said, one dark eyebrow arching upward.

He spread his feet wide apart and folded his arms over his chest. The pose made him look like a conquering hero, and her heart responded with an energetic and persistent thumping, like the damsel in distress she was.

"Obviously you have recently lied," she explained. "The fury of a thousand sandstorms has descended upon you and I'm caught in the cross fire. So I guess it's one down and 999 to go?"

He laughed. "Now who's revealing a flair for drama?"

"We're a pair, aren't we?" she said with a gusty sigh. Just what they needed. More air flow. "Just call me Sarah Bernhardt and you could be Laurence Olivier." A strong blast battered the wall behind her, and she glanced nervously over her shoulder. "Then there's the whole 'huff and puff and blow your house down' thing."

"A reference to the big, bad wolf?" His enigmatic gaze locked with hers. "I have heard of it. It's one of Hana and Nuri's favorite bedtime stories."

The supremely confident expression on his face was so profoundly male that her insides warmed and liquid heat melted through her. She voted him the sheik she'd most like to be trapped in a sandstorm with. Definitely big bad wolf material. And with every fiber of her being she wished he would sink his teeth into the role and kiss the daylights out of her again. Which was why she really, really needed him to go away and leave her to her book.

He stared at her for several moments until she finally said, "Was there something you needed?" The moment his eyes narrowed and darkened, she knew her phrasing was bad. "I…I mean, something I can do for you?" The suggestive words made her cringe. It was like being trapped in quicksand and every time she opened her mouth it sucked her farther down. "Why are you here?" she finally asked.

"As this is your first sandstorm, I wished to assure myself that you are not frightened."

The fury his closeness generated inside her was far more unnerving than what Mother Nature was dishing out. "I'm fine," she lied.

Just then a blast of wind smacked against the flimsy wall, startling her. She jumped off the sofa, moving farther into the interior of her room.

"I see that you are not frightened," he said dryly, moving behind her to place his hands on her shoulders.

The squeeze of his strong fingers reassured her at the same time it unsettled her. The warmth of his hands touched her skin even through the material of her robe and spread heat over her body.

She swallowed and turned toward him. "It just surprised me. That's all. You can go. Really."

"I promise you, there's no cause for concern," he said.

"I'm not concerned." Then her teeth started to chatter, giving her away.

"I will stay with you and take your mind off the storm. Perhaps some wine would help?"

"I don't think so." Just what she needed, something to lower her inhibitions. She was already precariously close to throwing caution to the wind. It was a really bad idea to be alone with him, but his reassuring presence did make her less afraid. "If we could just talk for a few minutes. Idle chitchat would be just the thing."

"Of course. Let's sit," he said, urging her back to the low sofa. "What would you like to talk about?"

She gathered her terry cloth robe around her, flimsy armor against the chill wind and the power of his appeal. "I'd like to pick up the conversation we started earlier."

The sofa dipped from his weight as he sat beside her. He was close enough for her to feel the heat from his body and smell the uniquely masculine scent of his skin combined with the spicy fragrance of his cologne. The intoxicating mixture burrowed deep inside her releasing the flutters she'd just restrained.

He frowned and his forehead puckered in thought. "I do not recall. Which conversation was that?"

"The one where you refused to admit you're a softie."

"I admit nothing," he said, but humor warmed his eyes. "I will only say that I cannot afford weakness."

"On the contrary. I was there when you were giving out cash like it was Monopoly money. From where I sat, it looked like you could afford pretty much anything. And I swear you were enjoying it."

He rested his arm along the sofa back, his fingertips millimeters from her hair. "I was speaking figuratively. What I meant was that concealing flaws is a sheik's duty. The best defense is an impenetrable offense. In disguise, one can work freely. Don't you agree?"

Crystal stiffened at his words and pushed her glasses

up more firmly on her nose as she lifted her gaze to his. Had he guessed? Was he baiting her? A particularly noisy gust of wind shook the tent as she answered his question. "I…I wouldn't know."

"You are pale. Are you still afraid?"

She shook her head. "Not afraid exactly. Definitely nervous. This is my first sandstorm. And we're so completely alone."

"You have nothing to fear from the wind…or me."

"I'm not afraid of you. And if the rest of the world could see you with your children as I have, your cover would be blown."

"I'm glad you trust me. While you are under my protection, I'm sworn to safeguard you in every way. Your virtue is secure with me."

"My virtue and I thank you."

His eyes narrowed on her. "If you were a virgin, under El Zafirian law, your father could insist upon a marriage if you were compromised."

"Then it's fortunate for you that my father will never find out we spent the night alone together."

His eyes widened, revealing his surprise. "You are a virgin?"

She'd meant the comment to be flip and funny, but he'd taken her literally. And hit the nail on the head. Heat crawled up her neck and flamed in her cheeks. "This isn't something I want to discuss with you."

"But you were nearly engaged. How can this be so?" he questioned, searching her face. His disguise had slipped big-time because his astonishment was showing.

"It's so because I never slept with the man I almost married. Or anyone else," she added, lowering her gaze as humiliation cranked up the temperature in her cheeks.

"Why?"

She *so* didn't want to have this conversation. But the fierce gleam in his eyes and the commanding tone in his voice told her he wasn't going to let it drop. "There was something about him I didn't trust. And it turned out I was right."

"What did he do?"

She couldn't tell him, of all people, that she gave the guy the heave-ho because he only wanted her for window dressing. "He wasn't the person I thought," she finally said.

"Then you were wise not to give yourself to him." He reached out and touched one finger to her chin, urging her to meet his gaze. "We are indeed alone. But if you trust nothing else, trust this. I am an honorable man. I would not compromise you."

"Why?" She'd caught the "why" virus from him, but oh, how she wanted that one word back. Her voice sounded pathetic and needy. How awful was that?

"Because you are a virgin."

"What difference does that make?" Now it sounded like she was begging. "I'm just curious."

"As I said, El Zafirian law deals harshly with a man who would so dishonor a woman."

"What if she doesn't want to get married?"

"If the issue is pressed, there is no choice. It is the law."

"Surely there are extenuating circumstances. If she doesn't want to marry, she could keep it to herself."

He nodded. "But the law was written to protect women from men who would merely use them and cast them aside."

"Why would a woman want to marry a man like that, anyway?"

"At least it gives her some recourse—if she so desires."

"So if you—we—slept together, you'd be forced to marry me if my father insisted?"

"Yes."

"And you don't want to get married?" she asked.

"That is correct."

"Should I be insulted?"

He shook his head. "It has nothing to do with you. Each son of the royal house of Hassan is required to marry and provide heirs. Years ago there were very practical reasons for this. The mortality rate was quite high. To ensure the royal succession, it was necessary to produce many children."

"But medical care is far more advanced," she said. "In fact, your brother is building a brand-new hospital to expand the current clinic. Surely the mortality rate is much lower now."

"Indeed. But there's still the matter of tradition. Each of us is still expected to produce children."

"And you have done your duty."

"Just so," he agreed. "There is no need for me to marry again, and I have no intention of ever doing so."

"Why?"

His face turned dark, angry almost as his eyes narrowed. His voice was like tempered steel when he spoke. "I have no wish to bring up a distasteful past. It is dead. Just be assured that your virtue will not be compromised by me."

"So you wouldn't take advantage of the fact that we're stuck here for the duration? And unchaperoned?"

He shifted uncomfortably on the soft cushions of the sofa. "It stretches the boundaries of my personal principles to be here alone with a woman. But as you say—

we're stuck. The law does not forbid enjoying each other's company as long as the man does not press his advantage. Since I refuse to ever marry again, you have nothing to fear from me.''

So the mighty had fallen once upon a time. A woman had hurt him. She knew it as surely as she knew her name was Crystal Marie Rawlins, and anger simmered at the edges of her consciousness. The protective instincts she'd only experienced with his children widened to include him. She wanted to smooth away the frown lines between his brows and the angry scowl from his mouth. It had been soft and seductive when he'd kissed her. Would he feel that way again?

She had no right to such thoughts. She was nothing more than nanny to his children. And thinking that way was dangerous to her employment. She needed to focus on the big picture.

The wind howled outside, and pebbles battered the sturdy material roof over them. In an instinctive, reflexive response, she flinched and pressed a hand to her pounding heart.

Fariq took her fingers into his own. ''Your hand is cold. You are still afraid.''

''No, I—''

''Do not lie,'' he warned. ''You are not good at it.''

That was unfortunate. ''Okay. You're right. I'm still afraid.''

His smile was reassuring with a dash of arrogance around the edges. ''I know. But there is no reason to be.''

''The wind makes me nervous. Any second I expect the walls to blow in. I have this image of being buried alive under tons of sand. A thousand years from now an archaeologist will find my bones and not know what to make of me.''

''I'm sure that won't happen,'' he said, his mouth twitching.

''Which part? The walls blowing in or the archaeologist?''

''Both. I assure you, I have endured storms far more intense than this one.'' He rubbed his thumb back and forth across her knuckles in an erotic, arousing, mesmerizing motion. ''How can I help? Name it and I will take your mind off the wind outside. Tell me how I can calm your fears.''

''Kiss me.''

Oh, Lord, she'd actually said it. Because she'd just been thinking about his mouth. And how soft and wonderful his kiss had been, once upon a time.

He looked momentarily taken aback by the request. Then, he smiled. Before she could say ''gotcha'' and weasel out of the humiliation her mouth had landed her in, he slid his arm around her shoulders and cupped her cheek in his other palm.

''As you wish,'' he whispered, lowering his head toward her.

Her eyes drifted shut, but the rest of her senses waited in a heightened state of awareness. When his lips took hers, a small sigh of satisfaction escaped. She felt the cushions dip as he moved closer, urging her against him as the heat of their bodies joined and fused them together. With her breasts pressed to the formidable wall of his chest, she could feel his heart hammering. The discovery made her smile. So much for playing it cool. He talked the talk, but he sure didn't walk the walk.

He slid his hand to the back of her head, then applied gentle pressure to make the contact of their mouths more firm. She cupped his cheek in her palm and was instantly aware that he hadn't shaved in hours. The stubble scraped the sensitive skin of her hand and made it tingle. Her chest tightened as the feelings grew inside her. The tip of his tongue glided across the seam of her lips, back and forth, urging her to open.

Her jaw dropped enough to admit him and he filled her, capturing the moist interior like the conquering hero she'd pictured him to be. Her breath caught, then jump-started and grew faster. Liquid heat flowed through her, settling in her belly, then lower, between her thighs. As pressure built within her, she squirmed against him trying to get closer.

He groaned and raised his head, his chest rising and falling rapidly with his own labored breathing. Before she could form a coherent thought, let alone words, he put his hands at her waist. With head-spinning swiftness, he lifted her onto his lap and urged her back, his forearm cushioning her at the same time holding her to him.

"What are you doing?" she whispered.

"As you requested. Taking your mind off the storm." He lifted her hand and raised her palm to his lips.

"What storm?" she whispered as sensation started at the point of contact and zinged through her.

He met her gaze, his own dark and intense. "You are no longer cold."

Hot and cold, maybe, from the flash fire his touch had started. "I'm not cold," she agreed.

"Are your fears forgotten, as well?"

He was talking about her anxiety regarding the storm, and the answer was yes. He couldn't possibly know her fears about him went off the chart the moment he'd appeared in her doorway. The violent commotion outside was nothing compared to what was going on inside. Especially inside her.

"My fears forgotten?" she repeated breathlessly.

She'd kissed men before. She'd even met some who tempted her to go all the way, tantalized her into throwing caution to the wind. Outside, there was more than enough wind to throw caution to. And the temptation he presented was so much more than she'd ever experienced before. She'd never met a man like Fariq Hassan, mysterious, sexy *and* a great kisser. He made her want to forget everything, including the fact that she was nanny to his children.

Nanny.

The word made her sit up. He'd replaced the last nanny because the woman had fallen in love with a sheik and made a fool of herself. Crystal didn't want to be another nanny-notch on the collective royal belt. She didn't want to be another employee who lost her head over a handsome prince. More important, she couldn't afford to lose this job for purely practical, financial reasons. And she couldn't even blame Fariq. She'd asked for it.

"I'm sorry, Fariq. That was stupid of me."

"On the contrary. As kisses go, it was brilliant."

She shook her head. "I think you know what I meant. In my defense I can only say the storm has me rattled."

"Trust me when I say you have nothing to apologize for."

"It's late," she said.

"Yes." He slid one arm behind her knees and the other along her lower back and lifted her off his lap onto the sofa. "Will you sleep now?"

Probably not. But she nodded. "I'm sure I'll be fine."

He stood and moved to the doorway. "If you cannot—"

"Don't worry about me."

He ran his fingers through his hair and blew out a breath. "Very well. I will see you in the morning."

She nodded and then he was gone. But the heat remained. She dragged in air, a deep, unsteady breath as she tried to pull her wayward thoughts into some coherent order. Sanity returned slowly, but one fact stood out like a beacon in a moonless night.

She was more curious than ever about Fariq. About the woman who had turned him against marriage. He had a story and she was determined to find out what it was. Even if she had to pry it out of him. For the children, of course. And in spite of that kiss.

Would he have done it if he hadn't wanted to? Even to take her mind off her fears? Was he really that nice? She shook her head. It was probably just a guy thing. He'd no doubt already forgotten about it. There could be any number of reasons. Realistically, two people kissing in the desert didn't amount to a hill of beans in this crazy world. But the children did matter.

If he didn't come to terms with whatever trauma he'd suffered, he would pass the fallout on to his kids. She was too fond of them to see that happen. Any baggage they carried through life shouldn't come from their father. And wouldn't.

Not if she could help it. Not on her watch.

Chapter Seven

Restlessly Fariq prowled the rooms of his palace suite. A vision of Crystal instantly came to mind, her beautiful hair cascading around her shoulders and caressing her waist. The memory of her soft curves pressed against him made him ache. Was it only twenty-four hours since he'd held her in his arms?

That morning, the sandstorm had blown itself out, replaced by rain that continued all day. He'd sent for a car to take them back to the palace and personnel to see to the horses. But the previous night's events had left his senses in turmoil and him in a state of confusion.

He'd found being alone with Crystal most pleasant and almost wished for 999 more storms to keep them trapped together. So she wasn't as safe for him as he'd assumed her to be.

Even after their conversation had conjured memories of his wife's betrayal—her seduction to trap him into their sham of a marriage—even those recollections hadn't been enough to keep him from kissing Crystal.

Or prevent him from wanting to again. In spite of his assurances to her that her virtue was safe with him. Fortunately she'd said good-night or he would have been lost. It had been a bitter pill to swallow when he'd realized if she hadn't asked, he would have kissed her anyway.

Their journey back to the palace hadn't presented an opportunity to discuss this mysterious fascination sizzling between them. His personal assistant had accompanied the driver and brought Fariq up-to-date on business dealings in his absence.

But perhaps that was for the best. Crystal was his employee. Her living quarters were under his own roof. He could afford no weakness where she was concerned.

Fariq smiled as he recalled her words that he could afford anything. Would her face, figure and philosophies crowd his thoughts forever?

Perhaps it would be best to talk to her about what had happened. He set his scotch on the coffee table and turned down the hall. He peeked in on his children as he passed their rooms, then continued to Crystal's, which was situated off the balcony with French doors and a view of the sea.

As he neared her door, voices drifted to him. Who could she be talking to? Anger surged through him, tying him in knots. Instantly he went back to a time when he'd discovered his wife had been faithless. She had chosen politically high-profile partners who would bring scandal to the royal family if revealed. What chafed most was how well she knew him. She used his love for his children. She'd known he would do nothing to harm their mother.

Stopping outside the partially opened door, he listened. He heard Crystal's voice, calm and confident.

Just the sweet sound generated a yearning that rippled through him but he pushed it away as he strained to hear and identify her visitor. When he recognized Johara's voice, relief coursed through him.

"I've met him many times," she said.

"Alone?" Crystal asked.

"Yes. I love him and he loves me. My father and brothers would never approve. But that does not worry me. You see, it is easy to avoid discovery. No one pays attention to what I do."

"But it's dangerous. Don't you see that, Johara?"

He could stand by no longer. "Crystal?"

"Fariq?" She opened the door wide. Late as it was, she was still dressed.

"I heard voices." He stared at his sister.

Johara stood at the foot of the carved, four-poster bed with her shoes in her hand, clothes dripping water and dark hair plastered to her head. Crystal handed her a towel.

"What is going on?" he asked.

The girl stared back at him, her eyes huge and dark. "I was caught in the rain and—"

"Do not lie," he growled. The idea enraged him. "I heard you. You've been sneaking out to meet someone."

"Fariq," Crystal said. "Calm down."

"I wish to hear about the man your father and brothers would not approve of."

Johara rubbed the towel over her face. She pulled her long black hair over her shoulder and used the cloth to blot the excessive moisture from the dripping ends. Her dark eyes were fearful, but her small chin rose slightly. "He is of no interest to you."

"I will be the judge of that. Tell me his name."

Crystal toyed with the belt of her skirt. "Fariq, getting angry won't accomplish anything. We need to hear what Johara has to say."

He glared at her. "I wish only to know who this jackal is."

"That is something I will never tell you," the girl cried.

"We'll see about that. Go to your room. Father will wish to speak with you."

"Really? How novel."

He pointed to the door. "Go. And don't even think about sneaking away. I will notify security to stop you."

"I've been a prisoner in this palace for seventeen years. Now you have merely made it official." She looked at Crystal. "I am sorry to involve you in this trouble." Then she glared at him before walking out of the room.

The outer door slammed as he followed Johara into the living room and picked up the phone, punching in the extension number for security. When there was an answer, he said, "This is Prince Fariq. My sister is confined to her room. Post someone outside her door and on the balcony."

He hung up and turned to find Crystal staring at him, her mouth pulled into an angry line. "What?"

"I...I—" She huffed out a breath as she shook her head. "I don't know what to say."

"Since when?"

"Everything that comes to mind is completely inappropriate."

"I will not hold it against you."

"You know what? At this point, I'm not sure I care if you do."

"You are angry."

She laughed, but the sound lacked its customary warmth and joy. "That's putting it mildly."

"Why?"

"How could you do that?"

"I will do more than confine her to her room."

She shook her head. "That's not what I meant. I was trying to talk to her. I guess you heard enough to know she's been meeting someone."

"Yes."

"Well, thanks to you, now I can't find out how long it's been going on and what, if anything, she's done with him. You're the one who told me El Zafirian law makes mandatory a marriage between a woman and the man who takes her virginity." She cocked her thumb at the door where the girl had just disappeared. "Even if she wanted to marry him, you just humiliated her. Do you think she's going to tell you anything now?"

"Of course." He ran his fingers through his hair.

She laughed again. "I think she can outstubborn even you."

"She will give me the information or suffer the consequences." He hoped she would not call his bluff and inquire what the consequences would be. "She is behaving like a willful, disobedient child and the behavior is not to be encouraged."

Crystal put her hands on her hips. "Has anyone ever told you determination is a positive quality in an adult? Channeled properly, it makes a person capable of achieving whatever they set their mind to. I don't think it's especially helpful to stifle the tendency."

"Unless it results in defiance, insubordination and rebellion."

She walked over to the French doors and stared outside at the rain for several moments. When she turned to look at him again, her struggle to subdue her own anger was visible in the rigid set of her shoulders and pinched line of her mouth.

"Fariq," she began, "Johara is a teenager—not a girl and not quite a woman. She's a normal kid with normal needs who must come to terms with her life."

"She has her family."

"Does she? My first dinner with the family gave me a pretty clear impression of what she's been dealing with. No one listened to her. Everyone simply orders her around, tells her she's silly or finds another way to invalidate her feelings."

"That is untrue."

"No, it's quite true. And I'll tell you something else. She feels isolated and wants friends her own age. That's normal."

"Johara is a princess."

"Whether you live in a palace or a pigsty, if you can't find love at home, you'll look for it elsewhere. And she found it. But thanks to you, I didn't have a chance to find out his name."

"She is a member of the royal family," he said stubbornly.

"If you believe an accident of birth sets her apart from the average, everyday feelings and hormones of growing up, then you're the prince of fantasy land." She sighed. "You need to cut her some slack."

He let out a long breath. "I concede that what you say has merit. But you must understand that the accident of birth that brought her into this family means that she is held to a higher standard. With wealth and privilege comes responsibility. It is a standard we all had to learn."

"It's not a perfect standard. The royal family isn't flawless. You admitted that you hide your weakness. But I'd bet everything I own that when you're cut you bleed—physically and emotionally."

"No," he ground out. Fury flashed through him. "My beautiful, faithless wife cured me of emotional weakness."

"Oh, Fariq. I…I—"

"I forbid you to say you are sorry. I do not need pity. The past no longer matters."

"You're wrong."

"I am never wrong."

She sighed. "I think we need to agree to disagree about that. But don't make your sister pay for someone else's sins. Until you can discuss this rationally, we're wasting our breath."

He started to say he loved his sister and only wanted her happiness, but Crystal turned her back to him and walked out of the room. Perhaps that was just as well. He did not wish to argue.

No. That wasn't entirely true. When he sparred verbally with her, he found the experience invigorating. Trying but definitely exhilarating. He recalled admiring her because she was a woman who could think for herself. The scene they'd just shared proved that she was not afraid to tell him what she was thinking. But that particular trait in a female most definitely did not make her trouble-free. Meaning, the requirements his father had set forth for the new nanny certainly hadn't worked, because Fariq was quite distracted by her.

Next time he hired a nanny, he would remember to insert an age requirement to ensure that applicants fell into the crone category. He couldn't help being grateful that Crystal didn't. The thought unsettled him.

But just now he had a more pressing problem—the necessity of informing the king that Johara, his youngest child, his only daughter, his brilliant jewel, had breached the royal standards of modesty and decorum.

When it came out, he had a feeling Crystal would have a thing or two, or two thousand, to say on the subject. The idea made him smile. After the night he'd had, he wouldn't have thought anything or anyone could do that.

Crystal put down the eyebrow pencil and critically eyed her handiwork on Penny Doyle, Rafiq's assistant. It had been several weeks since she and Fariq had disagreed about Johara's behavior. He'd also revealed his beautiful wife had been unfaithful. They'd not spoken of it again, but she remembered now because she wondered whether or not he would approve of Penny's glamorous appearance.

The young woman had also applied for the nanny position, but she'd arrived in New York after Crystal had already been hired. Apparently, Princess Farrah had taken a liking to the blond, blue-eyed, cute-as-a-button kid from Texas and hired her as Prince Rafiq's assistant.

Tonight El Zafir in general, and Rafiq in particular, were hosting an international charity event to benefit hungry children all over the world. Penny was required to attend and was unaccustomed to doing hair and makeup of that magnitude. Since they'd become friends—their rooms in the palace were quite close and as Americans they'd bonded—she'd asked for Crystal's help.

Penny's high-necked, long-sleeved, full-length silver gown had been purchased on a trip to Paris. It looked smashing on her, and Crystal took mental notes for her

next update to her mother. How cool was this? The
country bumpkin from the Lone Star State was gussied
up and going to the ball.

"You look fabulous," Crystal said, sighing with
envy. "Has anyone ever told you you're like a shiny
copper penny?"

"No. But tonight I'll take all the positive reinforce-
ment I can get. You really think I look all right?"

"Better than all right," Crystal assured her. "I'm pea
green with envy." She'd give anything to be able to
wear a pretty dress, put on makeup and do her hair in
a style that didn't put a permanent arch in her eyebrows.

"Aren't you going?" Penny asked.

"I'll be with the children. Besides, you should know
the answer to that. You've been intimately involved
with all the details of the event, including the guest list.
And the way you look, you're going to knock Rafiq
right out of his royal socks."

"Really?"

Uh-oh, she thought. Merely the mention of his name
put stars in her eyes and pink in her cheeks. Penny had
it bad.

Crystal sighed. "Just remember, Cinderella. Life isn't
a fairy tale. When the clock strikes midnight, nothing
changes, not even the pumpkin. You come back to your
room, take off your makeup and go to sleep so you can
get up for work in the morning. Girls like us don't
marry the handsome prince and live happily ever after."

"I know." Penny stood up and twisted in front of
the mirror, trying to see herself from every angle. "But
for tonight, I'm going to forget about all that."

"Just don't forget to watch out for wolves in sheep's
clothing."

"Okay. Anything else?"

"Yes. Remember every single detail so you can tell me all about it later. I want to pass it on to my mom. Shé would have loved seeing this. She always wanted to travel, but she's recovering from a horrible car accident."

Penny's expression was sympathetic. "I'm sorry to hear that. My mother would have loved this, too. She passed away when I was just a kid," she said a little sadly.

Instantly Crystal felt awful. She was so terribly grateful to still have her mom and didn't know what she would have done if she hadn't pulled through.

"I'm sorry," she said. "I didn't mean to be insensitive."

"No problem. Besides, I'm grateful to you for turning the ugly duckling into a swan. Now I've got to fly or I'll be late," she finished with a grin.

"And I've got to get back to the children. Break a leg," she said. "I've always hated that expression. Just have a wonderful time."

Crystal gave her friend a quick hug, grabbed the cosmetics bag she'd brought with her, then let herself out into the hall. She felt the way Cinderella must have when she figured she wasn't going to the ball, just before the fairy godmother appeared and waved her magic wand. Crystal had no illusions about that. No fairy godmother, no wand and definitely no ball.

Still, she would love to wear something besides the frumpy clothes her disguise required. She'd bonded with the children. Everything was running smoothly on that score. Maybe it was time to show Fariq that she normally wore contacts, more flattering clothes and a different hair style.

She walked the short distance to Fariq's suite and let herself in. "I'm back," she said.

"We're in the living room," Fariq called.

She crossed the marble tile and entered the room, stopping short at the sight of him.

"Wow."

He stood by the glass-topped coffee table looking more handsome than any man had a right to look. He was wearing a traditional black tuxedo with satin trim, white pleated dress shirt with black, silver-trimmed buttons marching down the front, and black bow tie. Big bad wolf.

Just when she'd thought she was safe, he managed to roll her socks up and down yet again. Would she ever be truly prepared for the sheer male beauty of him? Probably not.

"Wow? This means you approve?" he asked, sliding one hand into his slacks pocket.

"I think you'll meet tonight's dress code."

The sound of sniffling brought her back to earth with a thud. Feeling guilty, she noticed for the first time that Hana was sitting on the sofa.

"What's wrong?" she said, instantly going to the little girl and pulling her onto her lap.

Hana snuggled against her. "Papa says I must take off my nail polish."

Crystal noticed makeup from the child's face left brown and pink streaks across her own white blouse. Her hair was curled and piled on top of her head with ringlets cascading down. Crystal lifted one small hand and saw the bright, hot-pink color on the tiny nails. "I see."

"I won't do it," the child said petulantly. "And I'm

never combing my hair out. Aunt Johara made me look pretty.''

Fariq went down on one knee beside them and reached a hand out to his daughter. The child ducked away.

He sighed. ''You are beautiful on the inside, little one. You do not need paint and adornments to make you that way on the outside.''

''No,'' she said. ''Nanny, tell him to let me keep it.''

Crystal met his gaze and saw fear mixed with pain and anger in his dark expression. Hana wasn't her child and she hadn't gone through something so painful she'd vowed never to marry again. Until she knew his story, she was reluctant to interfere.

She wrapped her arms protectively around the little girl. ''You know what? It's bath time. I'll give you extra play time in the tub if you run in there like a good girl.''

''How much more time?'' she asked, her voice muffled.

''How much do you want?''

''An hour.''

Crystal laughed. ''You'll turn into a prune. How about eight minutes.''

The small, curl-covered head moved in a negative motion. ''Ten.''

''Done,'' she agreed, laughing as she met Fariq's relieved gaze.

''I love you, Nanny.'' Hana sniffled as she slid down and touched her feet on the carpet. She glanced at her father from beneath her thick black eyelashes, but she wouldn't look directly at him. ''I don't like you, Papa.''

When they were alone, Crystal stood, trying to think of something to say to lighten the mood. ''An hour down to ten minutes. That negotiating went better than I thought. It won't when she's a little older.''

"I wish I could keep her a small child forever."

"She didn't mean what she said."

"No?" His eyes were bleak.

"In a little while she'll have forgotten all about it. But she was only playing dress-up."

"The habits of a lifetime are rooted in childhood," he said.

"I agree. But it's harmless fun. We're talking about playing dress-up. Little girls love to put on their mother's clothes and pretend."

"Hana's mother is not someone I want her ever pretending to be."

"Maybe you're overreacting about this just a little. My mother always said flexibility is the cornerstone of parenting."

"I have never heard that expression."

She sighed. "And you're so flexible. Who'd have thought? Look, Fariq. Parenting is like a giant negotiation. Kids will try to find your weakness, then go for the jugular. Your best strategy is to not let them back you into a corner. If you forbid them to do something, it's best to make sure you really want it off the table. Because as surely as you tell them no, it becomes what they want more than anything. I know it's easier for me to be objective. Hana is not my child but—"

"No. She is *my* child. And this is not negotiable." His black eyes flashed. "I must go now, but I will be back to say good-night to the children."

Crystal watched his broad back as he left the suite. Apparently tonight was not the night for her to lose the frumpy clothes.

Releasing a long breath, she thought about what had

just happened. Hana's play was completely innocent. For some reason, Fariq couldn't see that. She sensed his prejudice was rooted in pain and he was headed for an explosion. But she couldn't help him if she didn't know what had happened to him.

Tonight she'd been able to defuse the situation, but the time would come when that wasn't possible. She would go to the mat for Hana if necessary, as she had for Johara. But not without all the facts. And she knew just the person who could give them to her.

Chapter Eight

Crystal answered the knock on the door, not surprised to see Princess Farrah, dazzling in a black-sequined designer evening gown.

"Your Highness," she said. "You look fabulous."

The other woman smiled graciously. "The children phoned me and asked me to stop by."

"I know." It had been her suggestion. And she had an ulterior motive. Obviously, there was more to the stipulation of a "plain" nanny than she'd realized. She hoped Fariq's aunt knew his story and could answer her questions.

"Is there a problem?"

"Only that Hana and Nuri desperately wanted to go to the party. I couldn't quite make them understand that even though the fund-raiser is for hungry children, to-night's event is only for adults. I thought it might help if the party came to them. Or at least some of the prestigious guests. You're the last of the royal parade. You just missed Johara.'' Crystal heard the sound of running feet behind her.

"Aunt," Hana said, throwing her arms around the older woman. "You look beautiful."

Nuri stopped in front of her and checked out her resplendent appearance. "I like your dress."

"Thank you, children." She hugged each of them.

"I like it better than Aunt Johara's," Hana said. "But Papa doesn't like me to play dress-up."

The older woman frowned as she studied the little girl. "Your papa has his reasons for not wanting you to grow up too fast. Never forget he loves you both more than his own life."

Crystal put a hand on each of their shoulders. "Okay, you've seen everyone in the family who's going to the party. Now it's time for bed. Run in and brush your teeth, then each of you pick out a book."

"Two books," Nuri said.

"Yes," his sister agreed. "Since we can't go to the party."

"All right," Crystal sighed. "Two books."

"Ya-ay!" they both said. Then they raced from the room.

The older woman was still frowning when Crystal looked back. "Do you think I'm too lenient with them?" she asked. "It's just I know how disappointed they are about being left out of all the excitement."

"Because you, too, are left out?" the princess said, her expression shrewd.

Crystal shook her head. "It's not in my job description."

"You cannot live in the palace and not feel the bustle of preparation and sense of anticipation for tonight's gala. Surely that is difficult for a young woman to resist.''

"I'd be lying if I said no. But there's something else on my mind." She nudged her glasses farther up on her nose.

"What is that?" The princess met her gaze.

"It's about Fariq. Something happened tonight and—" The overhead chandelier in the foyer caught the flash of sequins on the princess' gown and reminded Crystal that she was all dressed, duds and jewels, for an international event. Maybe this wasn't the best time to talk. "I'm sorry. You have someplace more important to be. We can discuss this another time."

"Nonsense." The princess waved her hand. "Let's sit for a moment. I'll be on my feet for a good long time tonight and no one will miss me for a little while."

"If you're sure." Crystal led the way into the living room, and the princess sat on the sofa.

"I am. What did Fariq do? It has something to do with Hana playing dress-up, does it not?"

"Yes," she confirmed. Farrah was a most perceptive princess. "She was playing with Johara while I helped Penny get ready for the gala. When I got back, he was quarreling with Hana about her nail polish, hair and dress-up clothes. She's a little girl. It's what they do. I can't help feeling he was overreacting, but I don't understand why. I know he was married and his wife hurt him deeply. But he refused to discuss it, Your Highness." She linked her fingers in her lap.

"You're asking me what happened to him?"

"Yes. It's not curiosity, although I admit I am. But his attitude will forever affect his relationship with his children if he doesn't work through the feelings."

"I agree." The princess took a deep breath. There

was a faraway expression in her dark eyes, then she frowned as she seemed to be forming her thoughts. "Fariq was married to a stunningly beautiful woman who didn't know the meaning of the word *faithful*. Her exceptional loveliness garnered her attention from many men in addition to my nephew, but she agreed to his proposal. He believed she loved him, but after she performed her wifely duty and bore his children, she gave in to the attentiveness of the others. Always powerful men who were untouchable."

"Did Fariq know?"

"Not at first, but eventually he discovered the truth."

"So she left and he kept the children. That would explain her absence," Crystal said.

"If only it were that simple." The princess shook her head. "In El Zafir, when a prince marries, it is for life. He did his best to overlook his injured pride and go on normally for the sake of his children. She was not of royal blood and had no such restriction."

"She stayed and continued to be unfaithful?"

"Yes. It was obvious to all of us, even before they married, that she didn't love him. She was merely interested in wealth and position."

"What happened? Did he throw her out?"

"It was as if she was daring him to. But, alas, no. King Gamil and his brothers tried to persuade him to settle a sum of money on her and sever his relationship even if he could not sever the legal bonds. No matter what their living arrangement, he would be obligated to support her for the rest of her life. And he would not turn his back on the mother of his children."

"Then I don't understand why I've never met her. Surely she cares about Hana and Nuri. Obviously Fariq knows how important a mother is to a child." She missed her own terribly. If not for frequent phone calls and e-mail, the separation would be so much more difficult to bear. "He hasn't forbidden her to see them, has he?"

The princess sighed. "She is dead."

"Oh, my."

"She was killed in the crash of a plane piloted by her lover."

"Oh."

She sighed deeply, then stood and smoothed the creases from her gown. "So, you see, he has good reason to be concerned for Hana. He fears that she could take after her selfish mother. It concerns him that Johara's influence, no matter how innocent, could trigger inappropriate behavior. If he errs with his daughter, it is on the side of caution."

What a nightmare, Crystal thought. He was a man of deep pride and she could imagine what the ugly situation must have cost him. No wonder he didn't want to marry ever again.

Crystal accompanied the other woman to the foyer. "I understand now, but Hana doesn't. He still needs to balance his feelings about the past with letting her become her own person. If she's forced to pay the price for her mother's sins, she'll grow to resent him and rebel."

"I agree." Farrah smiled. "It is good that you're here. To help him see what he is doing."

"It's not my place to call him on it."

"But I think you will not let a little thing like that stop you from speaking your mind."

"You give me far too much credit, Your Highness. I can't afford to let anything jeopardize my employment.'' Including her growing feelings for her employer.

The kiss she'd shared with Fariq the night they'd been stranded in the desert was unforgettable. But she couldn't let it happen ever again. She had to walk the straight and narrow because the thought of her mother losing everything was too awful to contemplate.

The princess walked across the foyer and put a gloved hand on the doorknob. ''Crystal, you are wonderful with the children and they adore you. We are lucky to have you.''

''Thank you.''

When the other woman was gone, Crystal leaned her back against the door. She adored the children, too. Learning about their mother made her heart ache, for them—and their father. The man who was never wrong had been wrong in a big, public and painful way. It wasn't something he would easily forget. Heaven help the woman who wronged him again.

The thought sent waves of apprehension through her. ''Nanny?''

Shaking her head to clear it, Crystal looked up to see Nuri. ''Have you picked out your stories?''

''Hana and I have something to ask you.''

She felt a negotiation coming on. This handsome little boy would one day grow up and take a position in his country's government. It was never too early to begin his training.

''What is it?'' Crystal noticed his sister hovering behind him.

''We want to go to the party.''

''I see. But you're not dressed for the occasion,'' she said, looking pointedly at their pajamas. ''And you asked for an extra story.''

"I know a secret place. We can see what's going on, but no one can see us," he said.

She nodded. "That takes care of one problem."

"Hana and I will give up our extra story if you will let us spy on the party."

"How about if we skip story time tonight. We'll go check out what's going on, then right to bed. No discussion."

He grinned. "All right."

He was going to be a tough negotiator some day. Especially if his opponent was female. "Go put on your robes."

As the children scurried to do as she'd asked, Crystal found she was excited, too. When the two returned, Nuri led them down the stairs and through a series of hallways and doors. He explained that there were many places to hide in the palace. Crystal lost her bearings and hoped he had a better sense of direction than she did. But finally they came out on a balcony above the grand ballroom. Velvet curtains framed the alcove, and a teak handrail with white spindles below it blocked the opening.

"Well done," Crystal told the boy. He grinned at her, and when he held up his hand she gave him a high-five. She sat on the floor and pulled each of the children down beside her. "We don't want anyone to spot us."

Peeking through the spindles, they observed the activity below. Muted sounds of music and voices drifted up to them as tuxedoed men and gorgeous women in evening gowns milled around the huge room below. Even from this distance, she could see the priceless jewels they wore. Carrying silver trays with champagne and hors d'oeuvres, white-jacketed servers moved smoothly among the guests.

"Look, Nanny, there is Uncle Kamal," Hana pointed out.

She spotted the Crown Prince smiling at a beautiful, dark-haired woman. The man rarely smiled, which made her wonder about the woman. "I see. And there's your grandfather, and your Aunt Farrah."

"I see Uncle Rafiq," Nuri said. "He's talking to Penny Doyle."

"I like her," Hana commented.

Crystal liked her, too, and hoped she was having a wonderful time. But it was important for her to keep in mind that tomorrow she would go back to being Rafiq's assistant. Because even from here the gleam in the prince's eyes when he looked at her was unmistakable.

"I do not see Aunt Johara," Hana said.

"Or Papa," Nuri commented, searching the crowd below.

The door behind them opened. "What have we here?"

Fariq's deep voice raised goose bumps on Crystal's arms as a tingle of awareness shimmied up and down her spine. Followed quickly by worry. Was this against palace policy? Would he be angry that not only did she permit the children to spy on the party, she'd initiated the peeping expedition.

"Hello, Papa," Nuri said, standing. "We wanted to see the party so I showed Nanny how to get here."

"I see."

Crystal got to her feet. She pulled Hana up with her and the child nestled close. "There was a grinding negotiation session. They gave up bedtime stories and agreed to go right to sleep without further discussion if they could see what was going on."

"I see."

"I hope you're not mad. It seemed—"

"I'm not." His gaze strayed to his daughter, who wouldn't look at him.

Crystal had the feeling he'd been on his way to make amends with the little girl. "I'll take them back to their rooms."

"Not yet. I have a surprise." He motioned to someone behind him, and a server bearing a tray joined them.

The young man laid out several linen napkins on the floor and arranged a picnic style feast for the two children. Crystal smelled the sparkling liquid in the flutes and grinned at the apple cider. On two small plates there was an assortment of appetizers. Then Fariq whispered something to the waiter who nodded, bowed and left.

"Thank you, Papa," Nuri said.

"You're most welcome, my son." He looked at his daughter and held out his hand. "May I have this dance?"

From beneath long, lush lashes, she looked up shyly and nodded, then placed her small hand in his. He urged her to put her satin-slippered feet on his shiny shoes, then waltzed her around the small alcove. A lump of emotion jumped into Crystal's throat as she watched him charm the pique from the little girl who alternately giggled and smiled adoringly up at her dashing father.

When the music ended, he bowed and thanked her. "Now, if you don't hurry, your brother will eat everything."

"Thank you, Papa." She reached her arms up and hugged him when he leaned close. Then she sat across from her brother for her share of the spoils.

Fariq leaned against the railing beside her. "Are you always so permissive with my children?"

"Only on special occasions," she said, glancing

down at the glittering gala below. "I hope the guests are in a generous frame of mind."

He nodded. "The Feed the Children Foundation will be well pleased with the amount of money we will raise from the auction."

"How can you be so sure it will do well?"

"Many of the donated items are unique. A song personally written by a well-known musician is expected to fetch over two hundred thousand. A limited edition Rolls-Royce probably in the six-hundred-thousand-dollar range. A weekend at a celebrity's French chateau. And that's just the beginning."

"Oh, my," she said. "Will you bid on the chateau for me?"

"Can you spare seventy or eighty thousand dollars?"

She touched a finger to her lip, pretending to think about it. "I'll balance my checkbook and let you know."

"Don't bother. I will buy it for you," he teased. At least it seemed like he was. "That will happen in a little while. Between now and then the champagne will flow freely."

She sighed, wondering what it would feel like to be able to afford such luxury. She would never know. All she wanted was enough to pay her mother's medical bills and get her back to normal. And a peek at the auction would be nice, too. "I wish I could see it."

"My aunt took me to task for not making arrangements for you to attend tonight."

Her? At the ball? It would have been fun. Dangerous but fun. She'd always believed character was more important than the way a person looked on the outside. But tonight she wished for a little less character and a bit more gilding of the lily.

"I'm just the nanny."

"Still, you are a guest in our country. It was remiss of me not to think of it myself. But I have taken pains to rectify the situation."

"What do you mean?"

"It was actually Aunt Farrah who spotted the three of you up here. She said Johara is not feeling well this evening and asked to be excused from the festivities. She suggested my sister take the children while I treat you to an evening of El Zafirian hospitality."

"What's wrong with Johara?" Crystal asked.

He lifted one broad shoulder in a shrug. "My aunt only said she was tired."

Crystal had a vague feeling of concern for the teenager, but figured it was merely her imagination running away with her. "If she's under the weather, she should go to bed. Hana and Nuri are my responsibility."

"She said she would prefer to care for them than attend the party. It is my wish that you let me escort you."

The door opened and Johara stood in the doorway. Their little balcony was turning into Grand Central Station, El Zafirian style.

"I will take the twins back to their rooms," she said.

"Are you all right? Maybe you should go get some rest," Crystal said, noting the dark circles beneath the teenager's eyes.

"I will see to these two." She smiled at the children, who took turns yawning.

"Will you read us a story?" Nuri asked, sliding Crystal a glance.

"Have you forgotten our agreement?" she asked with feigned severity.

"But, Nanny, I heard you tell our teacher that it is very important to read at bedtime," he said.

Johara took each of them by the hand. "I don't mind reading one short story."

"Papa?" Hana asked.

Crystal met his gaze and knew he was a goner. His little girl had him wrapped around her pinkie.

"One very short story," he said. He kissed each of them good night.

"Do not worry," Johara said. "I will care for them as if they were my own."

"Thank you." He opened the door and the three of them left. Then he returned to her side and looked down at the party in full swing below. "Now I will take you to the festivities."

Crystal glanced at the front of her skirt, the deep creases from a day's wear. On top of that, her wrinkled white cotton blouse showed the effects of bathing the twins. "No," she cried. "I look awful. I couldn't go like this."

"Then I will escort you to change your clothes first."

"But I have nothing appropriate to wear." This was Cinderella's worst nightmare. And not a fairy god-mother in sight. "I appreciate Princess Farrah's very gracious concern, but I have no wish to go down there and stand out like a longhorn at a garden party."

"An interesting image," he said. "However, you are far more graceful than a steer."

"But you get my drift."

"I do. And I had a feeling you might feel that way. So, there is only one solution. I will stay and bring the party to you."

The tingles sliding up and down her spine began to multiply as anticipation coursed through her. She should politely decline his offer, which was obviously nothing more than pity. Still, wouldn't it be rude to refuse? She'd spent an entire night alone with him in the desert and survived his bone-melting kiss. How dangerous could it be to stand beside him and watch the party go by below? The play-by-play in an e-mail to her mother would be so entertaining for her after painful physical therapy.

"Thank you," she said. "You're very kind."

Added to his above-average looks that made him a prince among men. And she could only hope she wouldn't live to regret this night.

Chapter Nine

Fariq picked up a bottle of champagne from the cart the server had just delivered according to his instructions. Alone with Crystal again, he was feeling quite content. It was expected that all members of the royal family would attend official functions. That didn't mean he enjoyed the crush of people, the flash of cameras, the attentions of social-climbing, power-hungry women. In fact, the longer he was not away on business, the better he liked it. More and more he was becoming aware that Crystal was responsible for that.

From the first day she'd arrived in his office, he'd been drawn to her, in spite of her unfashionable appearance. Or maybe because of it. She didn't fawn all over him, but spoke her mind and damn the consequences. As she'd once told him about balance, she was becoming that in his life. His children adored her. And he…he liked her very much.

Earlier, when his aunt had pointed out Crystal and the children spying, he'd felt an undeniable surge of pleasure. Since he'd already put in an appearance at the function, it was all the excuse he'd needed to make his escape.

He poured the bubbly golden liquid into two flutes and handed one to Crystal.

"To what shall we drink?" he asked.

She pushed her glasses up on her nose, then thought for a moment. "To understanding employers."

"I do not understand," he said, puzzled.

A small smile turned up the corners of her mouth. "I've lost track of the number of times I have overtly disagreed with you in regard to handling your children in particular and teenagers in general. Yet, you've listened to me apparently without any hard feelings. At least none that I'm aware of."

"Is that an apology for your behavior, Miss Rawlins?"

"No. That would imply I was wrong. I'm simply acknowledging I hold a different opinion of situations than you and you're gracious enough not to hold it against me."

"So you think I was wrong in the handling of my daughter earlier this evening."

"My mother always said don't judge anyone until you walk a mile in their shoes. I have no children and have never been married. I think," she said carefully, "I jumped to conclusions without all the facts."

"Your mother is a wise woman."

"Yes," she said. Shadows crossed her face as she frowned. "I find myself quoting her frequently. The children have noticed. I hope you don't mind."

"Wisdom transcends age, borders and time zones. Your father is lucky to have her."

She sipped her drink, then shook her head. "He doesn't any longer. They're divorced."

"I'm sorry."

"Me, too." She drank the remaining contents of her glass in a several gulps. "They raised five children and when I went away to college, it should have been the best time of their life. Instead everything fell apart and they found they had nothing holding them together."

"This was hard on you." It wasn't a question. He could see her sadness in the pinched whiteness around her mouth. "Yet you still believe in love, marriage and children."

She met his gaze, and doubts flickered in hers. "It's what my mother drilled into me. Do everything you want before settling down, she always said. Now I wonder if there were tensions in the relationship I didn't see. It's possible she suspected she'd never have the opportunity to travel as she'd always wanted. Maybe the subtext of her message was to see the world, live for yourself, follow your dreams because life doesn't always stick to a plan."

"Be selfish."

"It's not always a bad thing. I wish my mother had put herself first more often," she said with great feeling. "If she had she wouldn't be in the situation—"

"What?"

"Nothing." She shook her head. "You don't want to hear about this."

He lifted the champagne bottle and refilled only her glass since he hadn't touched his own. "On the contrary. I enjoy knowing more about the woman who spends so much time with my children. I find you quite a complicated woman."

"Please don't be concerned that I would burden the children with this—"

He held up his hand. "It never crossed my mind. You have defended them and my sister too many times for me to doubt your devotion to their well-being."

She turned away and leaned her elbows on the railing as she studied the party below them. "I'm in awe of the royal family's devotion to children around the world. This extravaganza is certainly proof of that."

"It is Rafiq's pet project," he explained.

"I heard. Talk about a complicated person."

Fariq was irritated at her tone of admiration for his brother. "Has he caused you distress?"

Just sipping from her glass, she gulped at his words and started to cough. He patted her back until she met his gaze. Lifting her glasses for a brief moment, she wiped her eyes. He got a glimpse of her without the spectacles and wondered what she would look like without the hindrance of them.

"Talk about jumping to conclusions. Are you asking if he's come on to me? Flirted with me?"

"Yes."

She laughed and shook her head. "I've hardly seen him. As a matter of fact, the children were just asking about him. They've noticed his absence. But the rumor is that he's preoccupied with Penny Doyle."

"Rumor?"

"Yes. News spreads quickly and this is all over the palace."

"What have you heard?"

"That Rafiq took her to Paris and she came back with a new wardrobe befitting her job as his assistant." She angled her chin toward the couple dancing below them.

"Including that fabulous little number she's wearing while he trips the light fantastic with her."

"She does look quite lovely this evening. Different."

"I heard she had a little help." Her gaze skittered away.

"More palace gossip?"

"You could say that." She finished the contents of her glass as she shook her head. "Look at all the amazing clothes and jewels in that room. What must it be like to know you can buy anything you want without thinking about a budget?"

Fariq had never considered the question. He'd never wanted for anything that money could buy. It was a privilege he took for granted, although he and his brothers cared deeply for their people and expended great effort to see to their needs. But he studied Crystal's tense features.

Resting a hip against the railing beside her, he was close enough to feel the warmth of her body and smell the fragrance of her perfume. The combination made him light-headed. Since he hadn't touched his champagne, there was no other reason for his reaction. "Tell me about your family. Was there a budget?"

She laughed. "So tight it stretched to the breaking point. With five children to raise, my parents learned to cut corners wherever possible. I think they were relieved when I turned out to be a girl because I wouldn't eat so much."

He laughed. "How did they cut corners?"

"Passed down clothes—except to me," she added. "My mother sewed a lot of mine, especially for—" She stopped and he was close enough to feel her whole body tense.

"What?"

"Nothing. It was just my activities—school dances, things like that."

He sensed that wasn't what she'd been about to say. Her nervousness was almost a palpable thing. "What is it, Crystal? What are you afraid of?"

"Nothing," she said with a too-casual shrug. "I was just thinking about my mother. She's still struggling."

"In what way? Is there anything I can do to help?"

She shook her head. "It's not your problem."

"But if it troubles you, it becomes my concern. As you said, I am an understanding employer. It is in the best interest of palace accord to keep my employees happy and content."

"I am content. I like my job. I've become very fond of the children, and it's my wish to remain for the duration of my employment contract."

Her frown belied what she said and he couldn't help feeling he'd somehow let her down. Then the last words sank in and brought him up short. Until that moment, he hadn't considered the fact that her time in his life was finite. It seemed she'd always been there and would continue to be. The idea of her leaving had caught him by surprise and was most unwelcome.

"And it is our wish that you remain—as long as you would like," he added.

"I hope you continue to feel that way."

"Why would I not?"

"No reason." She stepped away from the railing and set her flute on the cart. "I must go to the children now."

"But you've not tasted the food that was brought."

"I know," she said, touching a hand to her temple. "Two glasses of champagne are just hitting my empty stomach."

"You had no supper?"

She shook her head. "First I helped Penny with her hair and—" She stopped. "She asked me to lend her moral support when she dressed for tonight. Afterward, it was time to start the children's bedtime routine."

He remembered her comment that being selfish wasn't always a bad thing. He agreed. And it was time she took her own advice.

"You've had quite a busy evening." He took one of the hors d'oeuvres from the tray. "It is time someone took care of you," he said, holding the food to her lips.

The pulse at the base of her throat fluttered wildly as she took it from his fingers, then chewed. Was she affected by his nearness? He certainly was most aware of her, the curves of her body, the very female scent of her skin, the lush fullness of her lips. The musicians in the ballroom below began to play a lovely waltz.

Fariq held out his head. "May I have this dance."

"No, I—"

Before she could complete the negative response, he settled his hand at her waist, took her fingers in his and pulled her closer. Suddenly a feeling of rightness came over him. A sense that she belonged right here, in his arms. In the grand ballroom below them were some of the most renowned beauties in the world. Certainly the type of women he'd always been attracted to. For reasons that eluded him, not one held any fascination for him. Not one intrigued him the way Crystal did.

Certainly not because she was a classic beauty. Far from it. But maybe that was her secret. Without the distraction, he'd been captivated by her wit, charm and intelligence. The form he held against him was slight but softly curved and charmingly rounded—in all the right places. Her shapeless clothes increased rather than diminished his fascination.

He slowly led her in the steps of the waltz, grateful the curtains framing the alcove partially hid them from prying eyes. The opportunity to have her to himself was rare and beguiling, he thought. He glanced down, studying the alluring line of her cheek.

"Your face is flushed," he commented.

"I'm not accustomed to champagne." She sounded as if she thought he was displeased with her.

"That was not a criticism. The color is quite lovely and becoming."

She tripped, and he stopped dancing to steady her. "You're mistaken. I'm not lovely."

"On the contrary. I'm never wrong." He considered her features, especially her mouth. "The shape of your lips is quite attractive. My own still remember the exquisite softness from a night that feels very long ago. It almost feels as if I dreamed it. I wish to see if memory serves me well."

With his gaze locked on hers, he slowly moved toward her. Her eyes grew big behind the large glasses. Suddenly he wanted more than anything to see her face without the encumbrance. With regret, he removed his arms from her body, then reached out to grasp the sides of her spectacles.

"I have to go to the children." She gasped and backed away. Turning quickly, she left before he could stop her.

Fariq stared at the space where she'd stood moments before. She was afraid, he knew it as surely as he knew the sun rose in the east and set in the west. Her fears could have something to do with her mother as she'd said. But there was more. He very much wished to know what it was. More than that, he desired to have her confide in him.

"Cinderella and the prince lived happily ever after." Crystal sat beside Hana's bed and closed the book. Glancing at the little girl, she saw that her eyes were closed and hoped she'd finally settled down after all the excitement. When a shadow appeared in the hall behind her, she knew who it was. She'd only left him a short time ago.

Hana's eyes popped open. "Papa. You're back."

He came into the room and stopped beside the bed. "Yes. I came to check on you. You should be asleep like your brother."

"I was too excited to sleep. Nanny read me a story. About Cinderella."

"Did she?" He reached down and tenderly brushed the child's hair off her cheek.

Crystal tried not to breathe in his intoxicating fragrance, but it was a losing battle because sooner or later she had to take in air or keel over and try to explain why. Sustaining a normal heartbeat when she was this close to him was next to impossible. A short while ago, she'd been in his arms. Dancing. Just the two of them. She could have stayed there forever. Then he'd gone and tried to take off her glasses. To kiss her.

As desperately as she'd wanted that kiss, she couldn't let him see her without the spectacles. She couldn't take the chance of blowing her cover. There was too much at stake.

"Nanny?"

"Yes, sweetie?"

"My papa is a prince. Do you think him handsome? Like the one in the story?"

"What do you think?" she asked.

The child shrugged. "I do not know. He's just Papa."

What was she supposed to say with her boss standing right there? "He's definitely a prince."

His face was bathed in shadow, but she clearly heard his chuckle. "How diplomatic."

"In the story," the child continued, "Cinderella was the maid and she married the prince." Sleepily she turned on her side and snuggled into the covers. "Maybe you should marry my papa so you can stay here forever," she finished on a wide yawn as her eyes drifted shut.

Crystal adjusted the blanket around her. When Hana didn't stir, she turned off the light, and together they left the room.

"Good night," she said to Fariq and started to turn toward her own bedroom.

"I wish to speak with you," he said.

"Very well." She followed him into the living room and he motioned for her to sit on the sofa. Was she in trouble? For something other than the way she felt about him that is. Was he angry because his daughter's routine had been disrupted?

"I'm sorry Hana was still awake," she said. "I shouldn't have allowed the stimulation of seeing the party so close to bedtime."

"On the contrary. When she is a bit older, she and Nuri will be expected to put in an appearance at functions of this kind. It is wise to expose her to them."

He took off his tuxedo jacket and slipped it over one of the dining room chairs. Then he removed his cuff links from his shirt and rolled up the white sleeves to just below his elbows. After loosening his black tie, he let the ends dangle. It was a good look, a sexy-dashing-masculine look. Quite simply, he took her breath away.

She couldn't take her eyes off his mouth, the sensual curve of his upper lip with a dollop of arrogance thrown in. She had desperately wanted to kiss him again tonight. It had taken every ounce of willpower to walk away earlier. Something was going on between them, and she couldn't rationalize any longer what it was. But she wanted to tell him the truth so they could explore this attraction. Could she take the chance of losing such a well-paying position? Was it really a risk now? He had to know she was doing a good job because the children were thriving. It was clear Hana wanted her to stay.

"About what Hana said a few moments ago," he started. "Regarding marriage. Have you been filling her head with fairy tales?"

A surge of anger swept away her foolish, romantic thoughts. "Excuse me?"

"I believe the question was clear."

"First of all, I read to both of the children every night, books of their choice. It's well documented that children who are read to at bedtime become better readers and are more successful in school."

She stopped to take a breath and control her temper. She wasn't clear who she was more angry with—him or herself. Him for his arrogance or her for disregarding all her warnings and common sense and entertaining even the tiniest hope that fairy tales could come true. "Second, your daughter has a wonderful imagination all on her own."

"I do not ever wish for either of my children to be disappointed. But she will have to learn that things don't always happen as we might want."

"Of course not." Crystal was almost sure he'd been
sending signals that he might be interested in her. Hence
raising her idiotic hopes. But she'd have to be the queen
idiot not to get what he was about to say. She would
save him the trouble. "If Hana brings up the subject
again, I will make it clear to her that there is no hope—
No chance for you and me— There's no way I would
ever marry you."

He frowned. "No?"

"No." She folded her hands in her lap.

"Why?"

She raised her gaze to his puzzled one. "Because
you're not my type."

"Is that so? And what is your type?" Was there the
tiniest trace of annoyance in his tone?

"A man who's not you," she said lamely.

What else could she say that wouldn't make him
think her standards were a tad high? Because he had to
know he wasn't hard on the eyes. He was a wealthy
prince, a powerful man who was instrumental in running his country. He had a quick, keen intelligence and
a wry sense of humor. What's not to like? But she refused to say any of that and feed his ego.

"Good." He nodded thoughtfully. "I'm glad that is
the way you feel."

"Fariq, she's a child. The good news is she's fond
of me. As I am of her and Nuri. I don't expect anything
from you. Or want it, either," she added. "Princess Farrah made it clear when I went through the interview
process in New York that I was to always behave with
decorum, project a professional manner."

He nodded. "Your job is to keep the children safe
and happy. After that, your only duty is to avoid causing
any disruption."

"I know. Blend in. One doesn't do that and expect to attract any sort of attention. From anyone. Including her boss. When my contract is fulfilled, I'm going back home."

With luck, the money she was sending back would chase the financial wolves from her mother's door. As far as what Crystal intended to do after she left El Zafir, she hadn't thought that far ahead. She'd been too preoccupied with establishing herself and avoiding discovery.

She'd always believed that beauty came from within. She'd thought this was the perfect opportunity to take her philosophy out for a spin and see if she was right. And she'd felt as if he was responding to the her who wasn't a man-magnet. That toe-curling kiss in the desert was a big clue. Another was that near-miss kiss just this evening after dancing with him. But obviously she'd been wrong.

She stood. "So, now that you know I'm clear about things—"

"Don't go." He slid his hands into his pockets. "I need to remind you that I will never be so foolish or so weak as to fall in love again."

"I know. Earlier tonight I asked your aunt, and she told me what your wife did to you."

His eyes blazed. "How could you do that?"

She folded her arms over her chest and met his gaze. "You have emotional baggage that's affecting your relationship with your daughter. It's my job to know about it so I can help her deal with the ramifications."

"Such as?" he demanded angrily.

"The fact that she's paying the price for what her mother did to you. My job is to keep the children safe and happy. It's more than feeding, bathing and putting them to bed. They have feelings. They're smart and amazingly perceptive. Sooner or later Hana is going to wonder what she did that made you hate her.''

He took a step forward, and his eyes smoldered. "I love my daughter. I would lay down my life for her or my son."

"You don't have to convince me. But actions speak louder than words. What you've shown her is that she's in trouble for being a little girl, for playing dress-up. And there's nothing wrong with being a child for as long as she can. Children learn what they live. If they live with criticism they grow up to criticize. Once she realizes you already believe her capable of such behavior when in reality she's done nothing, what's to stop her from becoming your worst nightmare?"

"I will not let that happen."

"Will you crush the life out of her in the process? Will you drive her away? Like your own father is doing with his daughter?" She sighed. "I talked to your aunt because you wouldn't talk to me. I needed to understand your past to help the twins deal with it."

"There is nothing to deal with." He folded his arms over his chest. "I am their father. I will never marry again. End of story."

"And that's the example you plan to set for them? No explanation?"

"It's just the way of things." He let out a long breath and held up his hand. "As you said, we must agree to disagree. You cannot know how I feel."

"Maybe that's good. I can be objective because I'm not emotionally involved," she lied.

His already dark expression grew darker. "This discussion is over. It's late and there is nothing more to say."

He turned away and left the room. Crystal felt as if she couldn't catch her breath, as if all the air had been sucked out of her lungs. He would never see her differently from his wife. If all her hope hadn't died before, his last words effectively squelched it. Now she knew she'd mistaken an attraction between them—at least on his part. The only reason he'd ever been charming was to keep her happy and content. What was it he'd said earlier? A contented employee was in the best interest of palace accord.

She felt as if she'd gotten the one/two punch. One: no way would he ever want a relationship again. And she was beginning to realize falling in love with him would be as easy as single-handedly polishing off a half gallon of double-chocolate fudge ice cream on a comfort-food kind of day. Two: it would be career suicide for her to tell him the truth. If it was just her, she would come clean and leave. Because facing him day in and day out, knowing he would never care for her, not even if he knew the real her, was going to be difficult and painful.

But nothing else had changed. If she didn't keep this job, her mother would be buried under an avalanche of medical bills and could lose her home. Crystal wouldn't let that happen. She would just have to suck it up and move forward. This is where the character part of the beauty within came from.

She suddenly felt as if her boatload of character was going to sink her.

Chapter Ten

Fariq realized he'd made no move to touch his keyboard even though he'd been staring at a blank computer monitor for more than thirty minutes. Thoughts of Crystal had plagued him twenty-four hours a day for the past week, ever since the night of the charity auction. Abruptly he shut off his computer.

"Amahl," he called out.

His assistant appeared in the doorway between their offices. "Your Highness?"

He stood up. "Cancel all my afternoon appointments."

"Including Mr. Wellington? He grows impatient to meet with you and finalize arrangements for opening the department store."

"It can't be helped." He couldn't get Crystal off his mind and was most anxious to find out why. Unless he did, he would accomplish nothing in the office, including agreements regarding the exclusive store. "Tell Mr.

Wellington I am available for breakfast tomorrow, as early as he would like. Reschedule my other appointments, as well. If anything else comes up, one of my brothers will have to deal with it in my absence.''

"Yes, Your Highness.''

Fariq walked past his puzzled subordinate, then out of the palace business wing. He could understand the young man's confusion. It was extremely rare for him to cancel appointments, especially with a company that wished to bring business into the country and put people to work. But all he could think about was Crystal's courage in taking him to task for imposing his emotional baggage on his children.

He'd also been unable to forget her spirit, the way she felt in his arms, the reality that eventually she would leave and the abject emptiness produced by that thought. It bothered him more than he would have imagined. There really was no reason for him to give it any consideration; her employment contract would keep her here for several more years. Yet he couldn't seem to let the problem go. It was distracting him and beginning to interfere with his work. There was only one solution: he would find another way to make her stay.

But since the night they'd disagreed, whenever he arrived home she would disappear into her room unless he or the twins required something from her. He suspected she was avoiding him. He would put a stop to it.

"Perhaps,'' he said to himself as he walked down the hall to his suite, "a ride on horseback would be just the thing.''

The desert in general and the royal encampment in particular had fond memories for him since the night he'd kissed her there. Thoughts of a spirited ride with her by his side caused the blood to race through his veins. He would very much like to kiss her again and to hell with decorum, blending in and most especially, palace accord.

He opened the door to his suite and briskly walked into the living room. There he found Johara on the sofa with a damp cloth on her forehead and propped up by a pile of pillows. Her pallor alarmed him.

Quickly he went to her and sat on the coffee table beside her. "Are you ill, little one? Do you need a doctor?"

She opened her eyes. "I've seen the physician, thanks to Aunt Farrah. I'm certain it is just fatigue."

"Then you should rest." He took her hand in his, noting the iciness of her fingers. "What are you doing here?"

"Watching the twins. But they are with Aunt Farrah at the moment."

"Where is Crystal?"

"It is her afternoon off. I believe she said she was going into the city. To see the bazaar and to take care of a family matter."

"What family matter?"

Johara shrugged. "She didn't say."

His disappointment at finding Crystal absent was considerable as his anticipation of seeing her had been very great, indeed. But he knew the city well. Why couldn't he go to her? He was Prince Fariq Hassan. He could find anyone he wanted, especially his children's nanny.

He leaned over and kissed his sister's forehead. "Rest. I am going to the city."

A brief grin brightened the girl's pale face. "If I were you, I would look for her first in the city's financial institutions. She mentioned going to the bank. And Fariq? Tell Crystal I said hello.''

''I will.'' He smiled back, deciding against a retort. What could he say? He *was* going to find her.

Pride had made him harsh with her. When he'd cooled off, he'd realized she'd only been trying to help. But he'd lashed out because the debacle with his wife made him feel as if he looked the fool in Crystal's eyes. The absence of her good will had sorely tweaked him, and he realized he cared for this woman. He wasn't willing to think about anything beyond that. At this moment he only knew it was imperative that he spend time with her.

A lot of time.

With the information Johara had provided and the help of his security staff, Fariq found Crystal at the bank. He waited outside for her to emerge. The spring air was pleasant, not yet containing the heat of the summer to come. In the bright sunlight, he gazed at the pure white and light pink multi-storied buildings in the financial district of the bustling city. Kamal's plan to revitalize the capital was bearing fruit as numerous foreign investors and financial institutions located their company headquarters here.

Pride in the royal family's accomplishments filled him as he casually leaned against his Mercedes. When he spied her exiting the bank through the revolving door, he straightened. She wore a long navy skirt and matching jacket, with a scarf over her hair. Sunglasses covered her eyes. He waited for her to recognize him. When she didn't right away, he took pleasure in watching her look around, a smile curving her full mouth as she glanced at the tall buildings, the ongoing construction of new ones, numerous pedestrians and the abundance of traffic.

When she started to walk away, he called out, "Crystal."

She turned, her lips parted in surprise. "Fariq. What are you doing here? The children— Are they all right?"

"They're fine." He crossed the sidewalk and looked down at her. "Johara said I might find you here. If there is something you need assistance with I would be most pleased to help."

She shook her head. "I was just wiring some money home to my mother. It's taken care of," she said quickly. "Now if you'll excuse me."

When she would have walked past him, he stepped in front of her, blocking her path. "I thought you might enjoy some company on your afternoon off."

Her normally ready smile was conspicuously absent. "I don't want to keep you from more important matters."

Her tone would freeze water in the desert at the height of summer. Although the words would never pass his lips, he probably deserved it. He was too cynical. The children had trusted her right away and never wavered in their devotion. He'd been through enough nannies and should have known his Hana and Nuri recognized phoniness instantly. It was difficult to fool them because they were not distracted by looks or appearances. Now Fariq knew he must work diligently to regain Crystal's former good will. Again he wished for just a small portion of Rafiq's charm to accomplish this goal.

"You are not keeping me from anything. I have taken the afternoon off." He took her elbow. "Come. The bazaar is this way, just around the corner. I will show you."

She slipped from his grasp and took a step away. "I wasn't planning to spend time in the city. I need to get back to the children. Johara wasn't feeling well."

"Hana and Nuri are with Aunt Farrah. It is my wish that you take some time for yourself away from the palace."

"Because you're concerned that I might fill their heads with romantic notions and fairy tales?"

He stopped walking and sighed as he looked down at her. "You are angry. About the other night—"

"I'm not angry. Just trying to follow the rules and not overstep my boundaries. My opinion obviously doesn't count, even though I'm a highly qualified child-care professional. So, if you'll excuse me, I'll just blend into the woodwork and avoid causing a disruption here in the city."

"Crystal, I wish to restore the easy good-fellowship we shared prior to our discussion a week ago."

"Why? My job is to keep the children safe and happy. I know your philosophy dictates that keeping employees happy is good for palace peace. And it would make me deliriously happy to go back to the children. So if you'll step out of my way, we'll consider our good-fellowship restored." She folded her arms over her chest and waited.

"It doesn't feel as if we are back to the way we were. I regret anything I might have said to cause you distress."

"Are you apologizing?" The corners of her mouth turned up slightly.

"That would imply that I was wrong, which we both know is impossible." He smiled at her and had the satisfaction of seeing her mouth twitch. He hoped she would be unable remain piqued very much longer.

"If I were bold enough to risk my employment," she said carefully, "my response to that would be that *you* are impossible. But I value my job. Therefore, I will only say what my mother would say. 'If the shoe fits—'"

"'Wear it.' Yes. One of your mother's many wisdoms. Just last night the children were bickering and Nuri called his sister stupid. She reminded him that your mother always says, 'If you can't say anything nice, don't say anything at all.'"

"Or the ever-popular 'Sticks and stones will break my bones, but names will never hurt me.'"

"Just so." He smiled. "They are quite intrigued by your mother and her numerous sayings."

"She's quite an intriguing woman," Crystal agreed. "I miss her. If only I had half her strength."

His heart caught on the words. Was Crystal homesick? Would she leave before her contract was fulfilled? The idea was like a blow to the chest.

"Do you communicate with her?"

She nodded. "Through e-mail. Sometimes I phone. But it's expensive. I only call when I have to hear the sound of her voice."

"If you wish, you may phone her anytime from the palace. Do not fear the cost. As you said, I can afford it."

"Reach out and touch someone?" she teased. "Thank you. That would mean a lot to me. And I might just take you up on it. That would make the time go faster until I see her again. Just so you know, I recognize the peace offering and appreciate it very much."

"You are welcome."

He was relieved to coax a playful smile from her again. But talk of her mother distressed him, reminding him yet again that the time would come when she would return home to the United States. He found he didn't want her to leave. Not the children…and not him. Eventually Nuri would go to boarding school for his education, but Hana would finish school here. And Crystal was a good influence. The question was, how would he ensure that she stayed? Perhaps she would consider renewing her employment contract. Or—

Marriage was a permanent contract. It would also prevent awkward situations with other women that could sometimes plague him. The children adored Crystal. He admired and revered her. She wasn't shy about telling him what he needed to hear. And she seemed happy and content in his country. If he proposed, for purely practical reasons of course, what would be the harm? She'd said he wasn't her type, but changing her mind about that shouldn't be too difficult. And their union would prevent the necessity of finding another nanny to replace her.

It was a good strategy. The idea brought him more contentment than he'd experienced for a long time—if ever. It was definitely a good plan.

Crystal couldn't remember when she'd had a lovelier day. No matter what Fariq said, she knew he'd apologized. He hadn't admitted he was wrong, but he was sorry about the things he'd said. His sincerity was priceless to her. And the rest of the day took off from there.

He'd shown her the marketplace, pointing out scarves, leather goods and handmade jewelry. From one of the vendors, he purchased a sterling silver pinkie ring for her when she'd admired it. Then he'd taken her to an exclusive, elegant restaurant in the heart of the city for a lovely dinner. With candlelight.

Afterwards the driver of his Mercedes had returned them both to the palace. It wasn't a coach made from a pumpkin, but it worked for her in a big way. She would have to remember to tell her mother about how exciting it had been to ride through the capital city in such luxury. Now they were standing in the hall outside his suite. It was time to go inside—to their separate corners. They shared the same four walls, but might as well have been on opposite sides of the world because they were worlds apart.

"Thank you for a wonderful day," she said.

"It was for me, also. It is good to see familiar sights with fresh eyes."

"It's a beautiful city."

"I am most proud of what we've accomplished through an intensive revitalization effort."

This felt way too much like the end of a date. Thanking your escort at the door. Wondering whether or not he would kiss you good-night. In this case hoping he would and knowing it was forbidden. Quick, clean break, she thought.

When she started to open the door to his suite, he put his hand over hers to stop her. When she looked up at him, he rested his forearm on the wall beside her, leaning in close. Her heart hammered like a carpenter with a rush cabinet order.

"Is something wrong?" she asked.

"Quite the opposite. I just wished to say that I cannot recall a more pleasant afternoon."

"I was just thinking the same thing."

One corner of his mouth tipped up. "So, there are some things about which we agree."

"And many about which we do not," she reminded him.

He lifted one broad shoulder in a dismissive shrug. "Much good comes from discussion."

"I can't argue with that. Now we should relieve Johara."

The slight negative shake of his head and the expression in his eyes sent sparks of awareness into a wicked bump and grind down her spine. The only thing that made her turn away from him was the thought that they were standing in the hall and someone could see. Just as she put her hand on the knob again, she felt him release the clip holding her hair. The strands fell around her face and down her back. Before she could react, she felt his hand caress the back of her neck as he caught her hair and rubbed the strands between his fingers. Words of protest lodged in her throat, but when she turned, the smoldering intensity in his eyes made her mute.

"Your hair is so lovely. Why do you prefer such a severe style?" he asked. His voice was deep, rough like gravel and smooth as brandy at the same time.

"It's easy and convenient. Now, if you'll excuse me, I need to go in and—"

"One moment." He lifted her glasses from her face and tucked them into the breast pocket of his jacket.

She shook her head. "No, Fariq. Please don't. I can't do this. I can't lose this—"

"I can and I will," he said, then lowered his head.

All her protests dried up and washed away in a rush of passion so powerful it stole the air from her lungs. Crystal's eyes drifted closed as he touched his lips to hers. She'd wanted so much to know again the perfect pleasure of his kiss. But she'd never expected it to happen. He tunneled his fingers into her hair as she rested her hands against his chest.

With exquisite tenderness, he moved his mouth over hers. The touch was soft, gentle, but with the promise to take her to the stars and back. Where their bodies touched, sparks sizzled and arced and spread warmth over her shoulders, into her breasts then lower, between her thighs. A knot of tension coiled low in her belly, and she nestled closer to him, trying to ease the ache. Her breathing escalated, yet she couldn't seem to drag enough air into her lungs.

She slid her hands up and linked her wrists behind his neck as his arms tightened around her, drawing her closer, holding her to him. She could stay here forever. She never wanted to leave the security of his embrace, the tenderness of his touch, the pleasure and passion of his lips on hers.

He lifted his head and cupped her cheek in his palm. "Crystal, what you do to me. I have never felt such feelings. I wish to—"

Suddenly the door opened. "Papa, Crystal. I thought I heard you."

Nuri stood in the doorway. Crystal nearly jumped out of Fariq's arms and drew in a deep breath. Blinking away the haze of passion, she said, "Hi."

"Finally you are home."

"What is it?" she asked, walking into the suite. Everything was slightly out of focus because she needed her glasses. For her disguise and her vision.

"Aunt Johara just got sick. She's in the bathroom. She told me to get Aunt Farrah."

She looked at Fariq. "I'll go to her."

He nodded. "Yes. I will stay with the children."

Crystal hurried down the hall to the powder room

where she stopped and knocked. "Johara? Are you all right? Let me in?"

She pressed her ear to the door and heard sniffling. Then there was the sound of running water. Knocking louder, she said, "Johara?"

"One moment." Her voice was weak.

"What's wrong? Please let me in."

Several moments later the door opened. Fariq's sister stood there looking pale. "I am fine. I feel much better now."

"The children said you were suddenly taken ill."

The teenager pressed a hand to her forehead. "I...I think it was something I ate that didn't agree with me."

"Do you want me to call the palace physician?" She started to turn away. "I'll just go—"

"No." Johara seized her arm. "It's unnecessary. I saw the physician earlier."

Crystal tried not to jump to conclusions, but she had a bad feeling about this. The teen had admitted to being alone with a man. If anyone knew how easy it was to be swept off one's feet, it was Crystal. Hadn't she just allowed Fariq to take off her glasses, then kiss her in the hall? What if they'd been seen? What if he saw through her? She could lose her job. She knew better. And she had several years of maturity on Fariq's sister.

Crystal put her arm around the girl's waist. "Let me help you into the living room."

Johara shook her head. "I am fine now. Since you have returned, I will go to my room and lie down."

"Okay."

But for good measure, Crystal maintained her hold as she accompanied her to the door. She could hear Fariq talking to the children in the other room.

Johara opened the door and smiled wanly as she

walked through. "Oh, I almost forgot. The children
were curious about your mother. You must have told
them about your photograph album, because they
brought it out of your room and were looking through
it. We should have asked permission, but we have heard
so much about your family and wished to see the pictures. I hope it wasn't a problem."

Me, too, Crystal thought. Now *she* felt like throwing
up. "I'll go put it away." Hopefully before Fariq noticed it. "Feel better," she said to the girl.

After Johara left, Crystal turned on her heel and hurried to retrieve the scrapbook and photo album. It had
never occurred to her it would be dangerous to have the
thing. The pictures of her mother, brothers and their
families had brought her a lot of comfort during her
first days in the country when she'd been so terribly
homesick.

Rounding the corner into the living room, she saw
Fariq. He was alone and she absently wondered where
the children were. Their father was standing by the coffee table looking down at her scrapbook which he held
in his hands. She wanted to snatch it away before he
saw the truth. But the angry frown on his face told her
it was too late.

"Fariq, I—" She glanced around. "Where are the
children?"

"I sent them to their rooms. They looked through
your things without permission, and they are to think
about what they have done wrong." The frown deep-
ened. "Although justice does not seem to be served,
since without their transgression I would never have
known the truth about you."

"I can explain."

"Of course you can." He looked down. "So your

high school class voted you girl most likely to be Miss America." His eyes were hard when he looked up. "Was this before or after being chosen prom queen?"

"Please let me tell you—"

He flipped a page. "And here a newspaper article. You were a hometown beauty queen."

"Will you listen to me?"

"Why not?" he asked in a tone that said he wouldn't believe anything. "What's another lie after so many?"

Chapter Eleven

Crystal faced Fariq in his luxurious living room, the elegant glass-topped coffee table between them. The thick carpet beneath her feet made her feel as if she was floating. Or maybe it was the furious look that gave his features a dark, dangerous air making her dizzy. She wanted desperately to sit, but decided she needed to be on her feet for this conversation. This must be what it was like for someone whose life flashed in front of their eyes. Fear and dread twisted inside her as she realized she was about to lose everything she'd come to care about very deeply.

And more.

"May I have my glasses back, please?" she asked, holding out her hand. It was shaking, but that couldn't be helped. Her whole life was spiraling out of control. Maybe being able to see would give her the illusion of getting a grip.

"Don't you think it's time to abandon the disguise? Your secret is out." He glanced at the spectacles he'd hastily stuck in the breast pocket of his suit jacket as if they were a particularly creepy bug.

"*Disguise* is such a strong word and so negative."

"Yet so very accurate. You misrepresented yourself."

"I think that's an exaggeration."

He gestured to encompass her from head to toe. "So this is your usual appearance?"

That question was a land mine. "It is for this job. I merely pulled my hair back, wore no makeup and put on glasses."

"That's why you kept me from removing them. It was an effective mask. Because your eyes give you away."

Her heart was pounding so hard her chest ached. She hoped her eyes didn't give away the fact that she was in love with him. What a darned inconvenient time for that revelation. Because she had a lot of explaining to do if she was going to keep this job. More than on her feet for this, she needed to be on her toes. Maybe she could salvage the means to help her mother even if there wasn't a snowball's chance in the desert of a happily-ever-after with the prince she'd fallen for.

Slowly shaking his head, he studied her intently. "I do not know why I didn't see it."

"If you don't give me my glasses, I won't be able to see anything, period."

"So the story about your vision was the truth?"

"Yes. Normally I wear contacts."

"Of course." He handed her glasses over, but was careful not to let their fingers touch.

When his features came into clearer focus, she almost winced at the hostility swirling in his dark eyes. "Look, Fariq, if I was unqualified, I could understand why you're bent out of shape. But did I abuse the children? Neglect my duties, their care, their studies? Disrupt palace routine? Draw attention to myself in a negative way?''

His silence was answer enough. But it didn't explain the way his eyes suddenly grew hot before he replaced his mask of indifference.

''That does not matter,'' he said.

''Even though I'm probably the best nanny you've ever had and the kids have bonded with me, you won't cut me any slack?'' Frustration ballooned inside her. ''I have a very good reason for doing what I did.''

''It wouldn't have anything to do with wanting to marry a prince of the House of Hassan, would it?'' he asked, one dark eyebrow lifting.

It made him look bitter and cynical and she missed his teasing grin, his seductive smile. She felt guilty and awful for doing this to him. It never occurred to her that anyone would be hurt by her actions. If only he would hear her out with an open mind. Yeah, and the desert could expect snow in July.

''Marriage was never my motivation. It's much worse than that and not especially noble. Pure and simple, it's all about money.''

''Excuse me?''

She had the gratification of surprising the sardonic expression right off his face, replacing it with low-grade shock. He hadn't expected her to be so blunt. But the satisfaction didn't last long enough to calm her racing pulse.

She drew in a deep breath. ''First let me assure you that my credentials and references are all legitimate. I'm very good at my job and extremely qualified to do it.''

"Your competence has never been in question. But your methods are."

She winced at his icy tone. "When I arrived in New York for the agency screening process, the interviewer was going to eliminate me on the basis of the way I looked."

"So you saw it as a challenge?"

"Survival is always a challenge."

He frowned. "I knew you had a flair for the dramatic, but…survival?"

"I needed the money. But not for myself. It's for my mother."

"Really, Crystal. You can do better than that."

She decided to ignore his sarcasm. "My mother and father were teenage parents. They worked hard to raise five children. There was never anything left over in their budget for luxuries like trips. We all had to contribute in whatever way we could."

"So this disguise is the means you chose to buy them a trip?"

"Of course not."

"I see."

"No, you don't. How could you possibly understand? You've never had to worry about a mortgage, putting food on the table or paying tuition."

"No, I've never experienced those things."

"I wanted to tell you the truth. Many times. But several things stopped me."

"Please go on. I cannot wait to hear what was more important than the truth." He folded his arms over his chest, and the expression on his face was ice-cold and implacable.

She was dead in the water. But the truth was all she had, and he was going to hear it. "I fell in love with the children and they liked me, too. They were born into a privileged life, but it can be a burden as well as a blessing. I saw a chance to bring balance, make a difference.''

''Children are easily duped.''

Wincing at his choice of words, she felt as if she was fighting her way through the desert in a sandstorm. She wanted to shake him. But one look at his tall, powerful body told her that would be a waste of time and energy. She might as well just waste her breath instead.

''My mother always dreamed of traveling. She always told me to do everything I wanted before settling down or there would never be an opportunity. And it turned out she was right.''

''How so?''

''I was the last of five to leave home. When I was gone, my father and mother got a divorce. It seems after I left they realized the kids were the only thing holding them together.''

''Why?''

''Probably because they married too young and finally admitted to each other that they weren't happy. But my mother had never worked outside the home. In the divorce settlement, she had a choice of going to school for career retraining or owning the house free and clear. She chose the house.''

''I do not understand.''

''She figured she was brighter than the average untrained bear and could support herself with an unskilled low-paying job. But she didn't want to leave her home, the place where she'd raised her five kids.''

''I see.'' He looked at her and held up his hand. ''It's not that I see precisely, it just means go on with your story.''

His voice held just a hint of sarcasm, and his lips twisted scornfully on the word *story*. Crystal sighed, wondering why she bothered. Maybe if his wife hadn't put him through the wringer there was a chance he would believe her. But Crystal was paying the price for what the other woman had done.

She tossed a long strand of hair over her shoulder. It felt good to have it long and loose again, not pulled back so tightly. Every cloud had a silver lining, maybe that was hers. In fact, she found it liberating to finally come clean. The burden of her secret had weighed heavily on her. Unfortunately, her mother would probably have to suffer for Crystal's error in judgment.

"Mom was getting on with her life alone and doing fine. Until the accident. She was hit by a drunk driver." The look on his face was skeptical, and her own anger ignited. "It's a matter of public record. The case is still pending in the courts. Check it out."

"I will."

She glared at him. "My mother was hit head-on. She was in a coma, and we thought she was going to die. Finally she regained consciousness, and the doctors said she would live. That was when the real trauma started."

"How so?" he asked, studying her intently.

"Her care was expensive and she had no medical insurance. It was offered at her job but she couldn't afford the deduction from her paycheck. If I'd known, I would have done something. But she never said a word."

"I do not understand what this has to do with the fact that you deliberately deceived me."

"No, you wouldn't. Because you've always had enough money. You've never had to sacrifice or struggle. Mom tried to see it as a positive. Before high school when the boys noticed me, girls made fun of my clothes or my glasses, and Mom would say, 'Chin up, Crystal. Beauty is only skin-deep. Real beauty is on the inside. Hardship builds character.'"

Tears stung her eyes as she remembered the difficulties her mother had endured—her swollen, bruised face. The excruciating pain of getting out of bed. Crystal blinked the moisture away before meeting his cynical gaze. "My mother has more character in her pinkie than I'll ever have. But I like to think a little of it rubbed off on me."

"Go on."

She'd expected him to walk out by now. The fact that he didn't and still listened gave her hope. "Her recovery was slow. And she'll never be the same. She's still going through physical therapy and won't be able to work. But my brothers are taking care of her. Everyone is doing their part."

"Contributing," he commented.

She nodded. "Like we always have. My brothers are all supporting their families, so the financial part fell to me. There are several hundred thousand dollars in medical bills to pay. Or—"

"What?"

"She could lose her home." She swallowed hard and made sure her voice was steady before saying more. "I would do anything to keep that from happening."

"Obviously," he said. "Did she know of your plan to deceive me?"

"No," she admitted. "When I was looking for work, I came across this job, and I didn't know about the stipulation for a plain nanny until the agency clued me in. Because I had such a strong early-childhood-education background, they gave me another interview.

I toned down my appearance and was accepted as a candidate. Your aunt hired me. But my mother only knew the opportunity involved travel and she was very excited. The salary was so much more than I could earn in the States, and I desperately needed the money to help her. She put her dreams on hold for her children. How could I not put my dreams on hold for her?"

"So she would have approved of your methods to obtain employment?"

She shook her head. "She wouldn't condone anything less than the absolute truth."

"That is something on which we agree." His eyes smoldered with anger. "You could not have obtained a loan?"

She shook her head. "I don't have enough collateral to borrow the amount of money I needed to pay off the debt."

"I do not believe that the end justifies the means."

"But there's nothing intrinsically wrong with the means I used." She lifted her chin and squarely met his gaze as her anger kicked up again. "I know this is a stretch for you, but put yourself in my position. If your father or brothers or Princess Farrah needed something— If either of your children was in trouble and this was the only way to get it, wouldn't you have done the same thing?"

"No."

"How can you say that?" Her hands started to shake. Frustration knotted inside her because she couldn't make him understand.

"Because it's wrong. Your actions are fundamentally dishonest." He ran his fingers through his hair. "However, if you had been completely honest about your motives, I have every reason to believe my aunt would have chosen you for the position. Your work history and references are impeccable.''

She shook her head. ''I couldn't take the chance. But I've always believed beauty comes from within. This was a chance to see if I could be valued for my character and intelligence.''

''Why would there be any question?''

''Oh, please. We wouldn't be here now if it wasn't for that ridiculous qualification of a 'plain' nanny. All the men in your family see beauty as a distraction instead of an asset. You're just like—'' She sighed and shook her head.

''Who?'' he asked sharply.

''I don't want to talk about it.''

''I wish to hear.''

As she met his gaze, another of her mother's sayings went through her mind. ''Do as I say, not as I do.'' How could she encourage him to open up if she was unwilling?

''You know I was engaged. Before him, I thought only men having a midlife crisis wanted a trophy wife. I was wrong. He thought I would make the perfect wife for a man on his way up the corporate ladder. At a party I had the audacity to voice my opinion. He took me aside and told me to keep my mouth shut and just stand there and look pretty.''

''Obviously, he was a swine.''

The memory churned up the anger and humiliation all over again. She drew in a calming breath as she met Fariq's gaze.

''Obviously,'' she said dryly. ''But the point is, from my first day here, no one cared about the way I looked. The children took to me and I came to care for them. You and I have talked about many things including politics, finance and education. You'll deny it, but I believe you respect my opinion. I was valued for my character and intelligence, not the way I looked. And I discovered something completely unexpected about you.''

That startled him. ''What did you discover?''

''You're a nice man.''

''Flattery will not aid your cause.''

''You liked me in spite of the fact that I wasn't pretty. Do you have any idea how much that means to me?''

He shifted his feet. ''You're mistaken.''

''Really? Then would you care to explain that kiss a little while ago?''

''I do not have to explain anything.''

She put her hands on her hips. ''Must be nice to be a prince, to hide behind a throne when someone turns up the heat.''

''Hiding is your specialty, not mine.''

''I was completely myself with you. You once said there is strength in disguise. When I came here, I had to excel without props, rely on depth of character and internal fortitude. I wasn't anything close to your type, but you paid attention to me. You tracked me down in the city today. *You* kissed *me*,'' she pointed out.

''That was before I knew you were an illusion,'' he said.

She threw up her hands and huffed out a breath. ''You refuse to understand because you're angry. But if you were honest, you'd admit there are sparks between us.''

''Even if there was some truth to what you say, you have done an exemplary job of extinguishing them. My wife gave me one lesson regarding the duplicitous female nature. Now you've reinforced the message. There won't be a third time.''

"Then I feel sorry for you because you learned the wrong lesson."

"Which is?"

"Never judge a book by its cover."

The look in his eyes chilled her clear through to her heart and way down to her soul. "It would be best if you pack your things. Arrangements will be made for you to go back to America. In the morning there will be a car waiting to take you to the airport for the first flight available."

Even though she'd been pretty sure that was coming, his words were like a blow to the chest. It took all her concentration to keep the tears gathering in her eyes from falling.

She let out a shuddering breath but refused to look away. "Very well. I'll pack immediately."

He turned and walked away without another word. She couldn't fault him for not listening. But that brought her no comfort. It had been bad enough when she was only concerned about losing her job. But she'd lost her heart as well. She was in love with Fariq Hassan. By comparison, the fury of a thousand sandstorms seemed like a day at the beach.

The following morning, after being admitted to his aunt's suite, Fariq angrily stared down at her as she calmly sat on the sofa and sipped tea. How could she look so dignified, elegant and serene when everything was falling apart? When news of Crystal's charade spread, and chances are it already had, the palace would once again be in an uproar. And it was his Aunt Farrah's fault.

Before he could vent his anger and frustration, she

looked up. "You have obviously heard the news about your sister."

That stopped him. "What news?"

"She is with child."

He let out a long breath as he shook his head. "Damn. But that would explain her illness."

Crystal had warned him what would happen if the girl's needs and emotions were ignored. She was right.

"How did my father take the news?"

There was irony in her gaze. "How do you think? He is hurt and angry. He lashed out, and now he's backed himself into a corner from which there is no escape because he will never admit he was wrong or hasty. He's disowned her and will not speak to her. He says he has no daughter."

Crystal would say the king was "cutting off his nose to spite his face." Pain sliced through Fariq at the thought. He didn't want to think about her. She'd committed the unforgivable. She'd deceived him.

"I will talk to my father, but first I have some business to discuss with you, Aunt Farrah."

"What is it?"

"You've chosen poorly in the nanny you hired. I have terminated her services."

"Is that so?"

"It is. And when you find another, I suggest you thoroughly investigate her background. And she must be at least fifty years old."

"I had Crystal investigated."

"Next time you must dig deeper," he ordered.

She studied him critically. "I gather from the righteous indignation on your face you have somehow discovered that she is prettier than she pretends."

"You knew?"

"Of course. How did you learn of this?"

"I saw her scrapbook with photographs of her. Glamour shots. She claims she portrayed herself in this way in order to obtain employment that would allow her to pay her mother's formidable medical bills."

"It's all true," she said.

"How do you know?"

"I read the report." She looked up at him and shook her head as a long-suffering sigh escaped.

"Why did you not tell me?"

"Because the last time I checked, you were perfectly capable of reading it on your own."

A more important thought struck him. "Why did you hire her? She is everything my father was hoping to avoid with his specifications."

"She is perfect for you, something your father would not understand."

He blinked and shook his head. "*I* do not understand."

"Of course you don't. When the agency presented me with the slate of nanny candidates, they made me aware of Crystal's comeliness as well as her qualifications. When I met her, I was impressed by her spirit, intelligence and resourcefulness. In addition, I was deeply affected by the depth of her love and loyalty to her family. I was quite aware that she possessed outer beauty, but she has a depth of courage and inner beauty that are rare, indeed."

"It doesn't bother you that she has made a fool of you?"

"On the contrary. She did not dupe me. I had all the facts and made an exemplary selection. If she made a fool of anyone, it was you."

"She lied," he said, his temper rising again.

"No. You saw what you wanted to see. And you fell in love with the beauty of her soul."

"I am Fariq Hassan, a prince of the House of Hassan. I am too intelligent to fall in love."

But his aunt's words struck and opened a cache of feelings deep within him. Crystal had said much the same thing. But his sense of betrayal had caused him to harden his heart against her words. The truth was inescapable now.

He *had* sought her out. He *had* kissed her. He had wanted her. Even knowing her secret, he still wanted her. He ached to have her in his arms. Earlier, when he'd found her in the city, he'd decided it was imperative to spend a lot of time with her. He'd contemplated marriage as a means to not let her go. Although he'd fought against it, he'd known her mother's hardships were the truth even without his aunt's confirmation. But love? He was too intelligent for that.

He shook his head. "No. You are wrong."

"Fariq." His aunt slid him a pitying look and tsked loudly. "You are doing that which you so abhor—lying. Worse, deceiving yourself."

"Crystal is the deceptive one. And to think I'd considered marrying her."

"Aha. I knew it. If you cannot see that you are in love with her, you are a fool and I wash my hands of you."

"My reasons were completely practical."

"Good," she said, her voice dry.

Why did he feel the need to defend himself? "My children are fond of her. When her contract was fulfilled, I did not wish them to be unhappy."

"Fariq, I saw you kiss her last night. The children called me and I was on my way to your sister. That kiss was not the action of a man who is merely being practical.''

''It was before I learned of her duplicitous nature.''

She sighed and placed her delicate cup and saucer on the carved coffee table. ''You have been hurt. A wife's betrayal is like a knife through the heart. You are afraid of making another mistake that will cause you pain.''

He straightened to his full height. ''I am afraid of nothing.''

''Peddle it to someone who will believe you. You would do anything to avoid another blow to your pride. But it is clear to me that you're in love with Crystal. I know you love your children very much, but if you did not have romantic feelings for her, the idea of marriage would never have crossed your mind. Now you are searching for an excuse not to love her. This flimsy one allows you to save face, but—trust me about this—if you persist, it *will* cost you personal happiness.''

She was right. He'd known and refused to see for all the reasons she'd said. He sat on the sofa beside her and wondered how he would survive the aching void inside him where his heart used to be.

''She is gone, Aunt.''

''Gone?''

''The car took her to the airport earlier.'' He looked at his watch. ''The plane has already taken off.''

Just then the phone rang, and his aunt picked it up. She straightened, and a frown carved lines in her smooth forehead. ''What do you mean no one has seen them?'' She listened for several moments, then snapped, ''Alert the staff as well as security. The children must be located at once.''

''Hana and Nuri?'' he said, fear clutching at his chest.

She nodded. "They are nowhere to be found."

Fate had a way of kicking a fool when he was down.

Fariq fought the panic that threatened to engulf him. He would not lose everything. He would find his children. When they were safe, he would find a way to set things right with the woman he loved.

Chapter Twelve

Nuri turned his big dark eyes on Crystal as he held his sister's hand. "Don't be angry, Nanny—"

Crystal wasn't their nanny any longer, and the realization brought tears to her eyes. "I'm not—" she swallowed hard "—I'm not mad."

She opened the door to Fariq's suite and ushered Hana and Nuri inside. The royal limousine that had taken her to the airport had already left when she'd discovered the stowaways. If she hadn't sat up front beside the driver, no doubt she would have noticed the two rascals hiding in the spacious rear of the car.

She had to admire their resourcefulness and was proud of their intelligence. It couldn't have been easy for them to elude everyone and follow her into the terminal without detection. Her heart stuttered and nearly stopped when it sank in about the danger they'd been in, wandering around alone. She'd hailed a taxi and accompanied them back to the palace. Everyone from security to the upstairs staff had greeted the children warmly, relieved that they'd been returned safely. Obviously they'd been missed, and *that* was the reason she hadn't been turned away.

She looked down at them. "You must never do anything like that again."

"But, Nanny, we do not want you to go away," Hana said, moisture gathering again in her big, dark, red-rimmed eyes.

"Hana is right, Nanny. We love you. We wish you to stay forever." Nuri struggled manfully to keep the gathering tears from falling.

A lump clogged her throat at the way he struggled not to show his emotions. Someone had to teach him that men had feelings and it wasn't a cause for shame. Having them made a prince compassionate. Then her own eyes filled with tears because she wanted to be the one to teach him and his sister. But it would be someone else—someone who didn't love and understand them as she did.

The door opened behind them and Fariq burst into the room. He looked at her, then the children. "Hana, Nuri—"

He went down on one knee and swallowed hard, then opened his arms. They ran to him, and he gathered them close, kissing each of them. A sigh straight from the soul escaped him as he looked up at her. Emotions swirled in his gaze, and she wished she could read his mind. Maybe he wasn't so angry with her. But that was only her broken heart looking for a patch job that wouldn't hold.

Finally he set the children away and tried valiantly to put a stern look on his face. "You must never do that to me again."

"We're sorry, Papa," Hana said, patting his broad

shoulder with her small hand. "But we heard you tell Nanny to go."

"You were eavesdropping?"

"That means you were listening when no one knew you were there," Crystal translated.

"Yes," Nuri confirmed. "We were doing that. And Hana started to cry because she would miss Nanny."

"You cried, too," his sister accused.

"Men do not cry."

"Some men do," Crystal pointed out. "And it doesn't make them less a man."

It was the last message she would be able to give them but she hoped it would take root. She worried most about Nuri. If someone didn't show him how to open his heart, he would grow up like his father—afraid to take a chance on falling in love.

"Why did you run away?" Fariq asked them.

"We were going with Nanny," the little girl said.

"But what were you planning to do?"

They looked at him blankly, and Crystal sighed. "Fariq, they're five years old. They didn't think it through. It's perfectly normal behavior for their age."

"Unlike the adults around them," he muttered.

"What?"

"Nothing." He shook his head as he smoothed his daughter's hair from her face. He kissed the little girl again, then her brother. "Go wash up. Both of you."

"Are you trying to get rid of us, Papa?" Nuri slid his father a knowing look.

"What makes you think that?" Fariq's lips twitched, a familiar sign that he was having difficulty suppressing a smile.

"Because we are not dirty," Hana informed him.

"Remind me not to condescend to you in the future,"

he said. "I wish to speak to Crystal. Alone," he added when both children opened their mouths to say something. "Go."

He gently nudged them in the direction of their rooms. Impulsively Hana threw herself against Crystal. "I love you, Nanny."

Nuri did the same. "Me, too."

She went down on her knees and pressed both of them against her. If it angered Fariq, he could just stick it in his royal ear. The children had found their way into her heart. How would she ever get over the pain of missing them? And him.

"Do as your father says." Her voice trembled, but didn't break.

They moved toward the hall. If they'd gone any slower, they would have come to a complete stop. Finally, she was alone with their father.

"I was just leaving," she said.

"My aunt told me that Johara is pregnant."

Crystal closed her eyes for a moment and sighed. "I was afraid of that."

"You were right."

Her gaze snapped to his. She couldn't believe the words. "I take no satisfaction from it. It was this kind of situation that forced my parents into marriage and ultimately made them unhappy. It's why my mother was so adamant about adventure first, then love and marriage."

"What if love arrives first?" he asked, a gleam in his eyes. "And children?"

She didn't understand and decided he was still angry and was toying with her. "It's time for me to leave."

"Construction on the new hospital is moving well.

Kamal says it should be complete in several months. He is recruiting personnel to staff it.''

What did that have to do with anything? If she didn't know how deeply he resented her, she would swear he was delaying her departure. "I remember. You pointed out the American nurse at the charity auction.''

"Ali Matlock. Yes.'' There was a knowing look in his eyes but he didn't elaborate.

"Look, Fariq, I'm sorry about everything. Especially hurting the children and you. So it's best if I just go now.''

"Why?''

She blinked. "You fired me. I missed my flight because I had to bring the children back. But I'll get another one.''

"When?''

"Tomorrow. I'll wait at the airport.''

"Why not wait at the palace?''

"I don't think that's a good idea.'' It was a very bad idea because she wanted so desperately to take him up on the offer. It would only delay the inevitable. As her mother always said, "Never put off until tomorrow what you can do today.'' So today she would walk away and break her heart.

"I disagree. It's a fine idea.''

"Why would you want me here? You couldn't wait to get rid of me.''

"Obviously, the children were upset. And your mother's future—''

She pointed at him. She'd never held her tongue with him before, and since she'd already lost her job, she had no good reason to now. "Don't you dare pity me. I'll find another job. I'll help my mother keep her house.

I don't want my job back because you checked out my story and now you feel sorry for me.''

"Your mother will not lose her home.''

"Doggone right she won't.''

"I will see to it.''

"No, I'll see to it. It's not your problem.''

"What will you do?'' he asked.

"I'll find another job. Two if necessary.''

"I have something in mind—''

"What?'' She held up her hand. "No. I don't want to know. I don't think I can go through the interview process here again. Besides, with my education and background, I'm only qualified as a teacher or nanny. And you fired me.''

"Yes. So you keep reminding me. But there's another position that just became available.''

"As what?''

"My wife.''

Her legs suddenly felt like Jell-O. "Excuse me. I have to sit down.''

Instantly he was beside her, his strong arm sliding around her waist as he pulled her to his side. "Are you ill?''

"No. Yes. Maybe. I think there's something wrong with my hearing. I could have sworn you just asked me to marry you.''

"I did.''

"Why?'' She looked up at him, trying to read his expression. There was the usual intensity, but something else glittered in his eyes and made her heart beat faster.

"Hana and Nuri and I... There has been something missing from our life. I—''

"If this is about the children...'' She shook her head. "I love them very much. But I learned a lesson from my parents' marriage. No one wins if you sacrifice your standards and dreams."

"It's not about the children. It's what I want."

"But how can you? You think I'm a liar and a fraud. You have too much integrity to marry someone like me."

He dropped his arm and stood in front of her, close but not touching. "You were wrong about the lesson I learned. It's not about judging a book by its cover. It's about assumptions. I was so very sure you were no threat to my emotions. But with your innocent air and untapped passion you were a unique contradiction that forced my guard down. Then you marched into my heart and captured my soul."

His words took her breath away. "Really?"

"Really."

Happiness glowed inside her. This was a huge step for him, she knew that. But after what he'd put her through, she was afraid to hope too hard. She also wasn't about to make it too easy on him. Nor was she above wanting a little royal groveling.

"Why would you think I'd want another job here in the palace?"

"Because you love me." The corners of his mouth turned up.

Her heart instantly responded. "Even if you're right, and I'm not saying that you are, it would be stupid for me to accept."

"Why?" He frowned. "Do not say that I am not your type. You responded with passion and enthusiasm to my kiss."

"It's not that. You'll never trust me. Without that there cannot be mutual respect on which to base love."

"I trust you. I was afraid—" He stopped.

"You? Afraid?"

He took her hands. "I could face death without fear, but facing a future without you—" He shook his head. "Your wretched excuse for a disguise worked only because I saw what I wanted to see. Ultimately, it could not hide your beauty—inside and out."

"So you do love me?"

"I believe that's what I've been telling you," he said, an edge to his voice.

He didn't like being unsure. She knew that. Confidence wasn't as ingrained in him as he would have everyone believe. Now she knew he might put on a face for the rest of the world, but she knew the real Fariq Hassan. And she knew his heart.

"Actually, now *I* must disagree," she said. She didn't need to hear everything, but some things were essential. "You've been telling me a lot. But not once did you use the *L* word. I'd have noticed."

He pulled her into his arms and gazed into her eyes with an intensity that stole her breath. "I love you. I trust you with my heart, my soul, my children."

She melted inside. "I love you, too."

"You will marry me." It wasn't a question and not quite an order.

She didn't care. It was everything she wanted. There would be other lines to draw in the sand, but this wasn't one of them. "Yes," she said. "It is my heart's desire to be your wife."

"Good."

"So I can assume this is an admission that you were overreacting to my disguise? And you're apologizing?"

"On the contrary. I am never wrong. But it is possible that I misjudged the circumstances." His hold on her tightened. "I will say only this. If you leave me, the light in my life goes with you. You taught me not to judge a book by its cover or a woman by her beauty. It is purity of heart that matters.''

"And you didn't see me as just a pretty face. You taught me that love doesn't show up on schedule. When it happens, you need to grab on with both hands. Life doesn't stop because you fall in love. But loving makes the journey sweeter and more worthwhile.

A noise from the hall made them turn to look. Two dark heads ducked out of sight.

Fariq grinned at her. "I think someone is eavesdropping."

As happiness bubbled to overflowing inside her, she smiled up at him. "I think it's time to share the joy."

"Something upon which we agree. It gives me great pleasure to know that my children will grow up in a house filled with love. They will not carry the scars of my past into their own lives. And for this you have my everlasting gratitude.'' He slid his arm around her waist and nestled her against his side. "Children?''

Instantly they appeared in the doorway. "Yes, Papa?'' they both said.

"I have an announcement to make.''

"You are going to marry Nanny,'' Hana said.

"Yes.''

"Does that mean we can call her Mama?'' Nuri asked.

"If you would like,'' he assured them.

When they raced into the room, Crystal held out her arms "Group hug,'' she said.

Fariq looked into her eyes, and his own smoldered with so much emotion. "And so, it was written into the history of El Zafir that the nanny donned a disguise to kiss a sheik.''

Crystal met his gaze and smiled. "Let it also be written that beauty tamed the sheik after all. And they lived happily ever after."

* * * * *

Your opinion is important to us! Please take a few moments to share your thoughts with us about your experiences with Harlequin and Silhouette books. Your comments will be very useful in ensuring that we deliver books you love to read. *Please take a few minutes to complete the questionnaire, then send it to us at the address below.*

Send your completed questionnaires to:
Harlequin/Silhouette Reader Survey, P.O. Box 9046, Buffalo, NY 14269-9046

1. As you may know, there are many different lines under the Harlequin and Silhouette brands. Each of the lines is listed below. Please check the box that most represents your reading habit for each line.

Line	Currently read this line	Do not read this line	Not sure if I read this line
Harlequin American Romance	❑	❑	❑
Harlequin Duets	❑	❑	❑
Harlequin Romance	❑	❑	❑
Harlequin Historicals	❑	❑	❑
Harlequin Superromance	❑	❑	❑
Harlequin Intrigue	❑	❑	❑
Harlequin Presents	❑	❑	❑
Harlequin Temptation	❑	❑	❑
Harlequin Blaze	❑	❑	❑
Silhouette Special Edition	❑	❑	❑
Silhouette Romance	❑	❑	❑
Silhouette Intimate Moments	❑	❑	❑
Silhouette Desire	❑	❑	❑

2. Which of the following best describes why you bought *this book?* One answer only, please.

the picture on the cover	❑	the title	❑
the author	❑	the line is one I read often	❑
part of a miniseries	❑	saw an ad in another book	❑
saw an ad in a magazine/newsletter	❑	a friend told me about it	❑
I borrowed/was given this book	❑	other: _____	❑

3. Where did you buy *this book?* One answer only, please.

at Barnes & Noble	❑	at a grocery store	❑
at Waldenbooks	❑	at a drugstore	❑
at Borders	❑	on eHarlequin.com Web site	❑
at another bookstore	❑	from another Web site	❑
at Wal-Mart	❑	Harlequin/Silhouette Reader	❑
at Target	❑	Service/through the mail	
at Kmart	❑	used books from anywhere	❑
at another department store or mass merchandiser	❑	I borrowed/was given this book	❑

4. On average, how many Harlequin and Silhouette books do you buy at one time?

I buy _____ books at one time	❑
I rarely buy a book	❑

MRQ403SR-1A

5. How many times per month do you shop for any *Harlequin and/or Silhouette* books?
   One answer only, please.

   1 or more times a week ❏   a few times per year ❏
   1 to 3 times per month ❏   less often than once a year ❏
   1 to 2 times every 3 months ❏   never ❏

6. When you think of your ideal heroine, which *one* statement describes her the best?
   One answer only, please.

   She's a woman who is strong-willed ❏   She's a desirable woman ❏
   She's a woman who is needed by others ❏   She's a powerful woman ❏
   She's a woman who is taken care of ❏   She's a passionate woman ❏
   She's an adventurous woman ❏   She's a sensitive woman ❏

7. The following statements describe types or genres of books that you may be
   interested in reading. Pick *up to 2 types* of books that you are most interested in.

   I like to read about truly romantic relationships ❏
   I like to read stories that are sexy romances ❏
   I like to read romantic comedies ❏
   I like to read a romantic mystery/suspense ❏
   I like to read about romantic adventures ❏
   I like to read romance stories that involve family ❏
   I like to read about a romance in times or places that I have never seen ❏
   Other: _____ ❏

*The following questions help us to group your answers with those readers who are
similar to you. Your answers will remain confidential.*

8. Please record your year of birth below.
   19 ____

9. What is your marital status?
   single ❏   married ❏   common-law ❏   widowed ❏
   divorced/separated ❏

10. Do you have children 18 years of age or younger currently living at home?
    yes ❏   no ❏

11. Which of the following best describes your employment status?
    employed full-time or part-time ❏   homemaker ❏   student ❏
    retired ❏   unemployed ❏

12. Do you have access to the Internet from either home or work?
    yes ❏   no ❏

13. Have you ever visited eHarlequin.com?
    yes ❏   no ❏

14. What state do you live in?
    _____

15. Are you a member of Harlequin/Silhouette Reader Service?
    yes ❏   Account # _____   no ❏   MRQ403SR-1B